I0640959

Hair On Fire in the 50s & 60s

Joe Ruff's Exceptional Life, Volume 1

P.T. "Doc" Carney

Published by P.T. "Doc" Carney, 2018.

While every precaution has been taken in the preparation of this book, the publisher assumes no responsibility for errors or omissions, or for damages resulting from the use of the information contained herein.

HAIR ON FIRE... in the 50s & 60s

First edition. March 31, 2018.

Copyright © 2018 P.T. "Doc" Carney.

ISBN: 978-1-732208414

Written by P.T. "Doc" Carney.

Cover Design by Tiffany Fox

Copy Editing by Debby Gibbs

Library of Congress Control Number: 2018904817

TABLE OF CONTENTS

Prologue

JOE NEVER KNEW WHAT HAPPENED. He had lost a lot of blood. He never remembered being picked up by an American fishing boat. When he awakened, he was in the Eglin AFB hospital where he had been delivered by the US Navy from Key West. According to the fishing boat operator, he had been found floating in the ocean, appearing to them to be dead. Only after getting him to the dingy did the fishing boat captain realize that Joe was still alive. They rushed him to the Navy facility in Key West, and after transfusing 4 units of blood, they transferred Joe to Eglin AFB. Joe had no recollection from the time he hit the water until after the blood transfusion...

Chapter 1

Little Joe Ruff

JOE RUFF WAS BORN ON April 22, 1934 during the height of the Great Depression that started on October 21st, 1929. Joe's older brother was born in 1932 to the same parents, Bubba and Clarice Ruff, so the boys were about two years apart.

They lived in a tenant house on the grandfather's farm just south of the township of Meridian, Lauderdale County, Mississippi. Joe's parents, Bubba and Clarice, dropped out of school in the 10th grade when they were fourteen years of age and married amidst great anger for doing so. They felt so much pressure that they even ran away to Texas for a year where Bubba did farm labor to support them.

After a year of hardship while living in Texas, the two returned to Meridian where Bubba took a job at the one livestock auction in the area cleaning out the cow manure from the pins and helping on sale days with the auction of the cattle, horses, mules, goats, sheep, hogs, and anything else that the poor people of the surrounding area had for sale. You could never tell what someone might bring in to sell, from an old lantern to a bale of hay, to a gold watch, they would sell it at that livestock auction.

Bubba rode horseback five miles to work each day and back, six days a week for a dollar a day. They married in 1930 and by 1932 their first child, Brick, was born; so there was another mouth to feed. And by 1934, the second child, another boy, was born. They named him Joe.

Times were hard, but no one seemed to take it personal. There was very little or no money, and so it seemed that everyone was in the same boat. If you had rich neighbors, there might have been a lot of envy, but everyone was poor.

The Andrew Ruff family, Joe's paternal grandfather and grandmother, would go on to have four children in all, spaced about two to three years apart. The 2nd child was also a boy and he was named Ralph. Then they had the first of two girls, Penelope and then the last child, a girl they named Kathryn .

Chapter 2

Ruff Family History

IN 1938 GRANDFATHER Andrew Ruff opened a Live Stock Commission company just south of the railroad tracks from downtown Meridian, which in those days was called a cattle auction barn. They had sale day every Tuesday and were in competition with one other sale barn that had been there for many years, The Owen Bros. Barn. But Owen Bros. would soon close, leaving an unopposed market for the Dixie Stockyard. Joe's Dad was the Assistant Manager, later made General Manager.

Uncle Harry Curwell

Now Joe's Uncle Harry Curwell was a sight to behold. He was the baby brother of Momice Ruff, Joe's paternal grandmother . He was about 5 feet 6 inches tall, heavy set and with blue eyes. He was, no joke, the strongest white man Joe had ever seen and he could lift the front end of a Model T Ford off the ground. There was only one other man around the Dixie Stockyard that was able to do this, Lewis Harmon, who was also built just like Uncle Harry. Lewis also worked at the stockyard. Now HE was the strongest colored man Joe had ever seen.

Uncle Harry ran the check-in booth of the Dixie Stockyard, so when a farmer or rancher brought his cattle or hogs to the unloading chutes to sell, Uncle Harry was his first stop. Several of the workers would run the livestock through the chute and in the case of cattle, each animal would have a tag put in its ear, usually the left ear, for identification purposes. If they brought hogs, goats, mules, horses, donkeys or other animals, the number of them would be counted.

Joe remembers well that as a child he was allowed to work at the sale barn beginning at about age 12. Joe worked wherever he was told to work that day, and he never knew where they might need him on any particular day. On average, there would be 8-10 extra workers on sale day. There were maybe two workers who were there full time.

At the end of the sale, Uncle Harry would go into the office to the pay window and open the cash drawer and pay the help. Depending on whether he thought Joe had worked hard enough, he paid Joe two dollars for a day's work. The better and more essential the helper was, the more Uncle Harry paid them. As a general rule, he paid them from four to eight dollars for the day depending on how valuable they were. Now remember, this was in the 1940s, and that was a good day's pay.

One day a government official was there and asked Uncle Harry why he was allowing a child like Joe to work there. Didn't he know about the child labor law? Uncle Harry responded that Joe was working "so that he could learn to be a productive citizen and wouldn't have to grow up to be a government worker like him." With that, the man picked up his brief case and left. To say the least, the Ruff family believed that the less government governs, the better people are able to help themselves.

There was also a night watchman who worked for the Stockyard. His name was James Mattok and he came to work each day at 5 pm and stayed until someone arrived in the morning. He was a short, stocky man, but not as stocky as Uncle Harry. He never shot anyone on the job but he had been a Marine and served in the Pacific Combat Theatre in WW2. He carried a 38 pistol and knew how to use it. The Stockyard had a huge feed room located in the rear of the stock barn and all outside gates were locked at night. People in those days would steal livestock and feed though they would not break into your home or steal your car. They would also "borrow" firewood. So Mr. Mattok would fire his weapon into the air if he saw them on the property after dark. He made regular rounds around the Stockyard about every hour at night. Uncle Harry and Mattok were close friends and Harry spent most of his evenings there visiting. Uncle Harry had a long time girl friend, Goldie, whom he also saw; but he still spent most of his evenings visiting with Mattok. Uncle Harry never married, but on his demise he left all his estate to Goldie.

After Joe was able to drive, it was great fun stopping by the Stock barn on Saturday evenings to visit with the two of them. They told the biggest possible lies about when they were young, and especially Mattok, who told about his escapades with women. It was hysterical years later for Joe to remember those two guys. Mattok, again, was a little short guy too, about 5 feet 7 inches tall, with a stocky build and cool, grey eyes. It was odd, but those two, in time, would die close together. Uncle Harry died at age 60 of complications from diabetes. Mattok, on the other hand, died late one afternoon just after arriving for work. The office staff, including Mr. Hanley, the bookkeeper, and Jodie, the secretary, and Uncle Ralph were still there. Mr. Mattok hopped off the stool on which he was sitting, quickly sat down in a chair, threw his head back, and he was gone, just like that, at 65 years of age. Sadly, efforts to resuscitate him failed.

Uncle Ralph Ruff

Uncle Ralph worked at the Stockyard as well. But Uncle Ralph would soon go away to the US Army for four years.

Uncle Ralph, the second eldest child of Andrew and Momice Ruff, would grow up and graduate from Meridian High School in1942. In high school he was tall and thin and a member of the track team. He ran the 1/2 mile and was very fast. After high school, he attended LSU for one year following which he enlisted in the US Army. He remained in the Army until the end of WW2 and then returned to his home in Meridian, Mississippi.

While Uncle Ralph was in the Army he was stationed in Jacksonville, Florida, and at a social function he met, and a few months later married, a young lady by the name of Susan Zinc. She was short and slim, built like his mother. You know there is an old saying that Mama's boys marry a girl just like Mom, or in some cases they don't marry at all. Well, it's dubious as to whether this holds true most of the time, but it did play-out in this case . After the war was over Uncle Ralph did bring his bride home, and they moved into Northwood on the north side of town near the Northwood Country Club, where one could play golf and take advantage of the Club itself, but Uncle Ralph found himself working all the time, leaving no time for such leisure. He was, at this point, made Assistant Manager of the Dixie Stockyards a position he would hold until 1954, at which time he would step up to the Manager's position when his younger brother, Bubba, sold out one of his farms and moved to California. During his years of work he also opened and established an Office Supply Company, which went on to become a successful business. He would later sell that business for large profit.

Uncle Ralph, personality wise, was the complete opposite of his younger brother, Bubba. He seldom raised his voice and was a wholesome pleasure to deal with. Customers and friends alike adored him for his low key but businesslike manner. He managed the Stock Barn until it closed 40 years after it had opened.

Aunt Penelope & Uncle Bert

Aunt Penelope was born in 1923. She was the first of two girls to be born to the Andrew Ruff family and grew up in the same rural community on the Ruff farm. Later she was to be joined upstairs by her Grandmother Ruff, who came to live with her oldest son Andrew after Andrew's father had left her for a younger woman. As a small child, she had always clung to her mother and this would continue throughout her entire life until her mother's death in 1984. Throughout her life in grade school, junior high, and high school, she was her mother's closest companion and confidant. She was an outgoing person and a general jabber box. There was never a dull moment when Penny was around . She was very talkative, to say the least, but not offensive to most people.

After high school, Penelope did go away to an all girls' school in Montgomery, Alabama. While at the girls' school, she met the man who was to be her husband for life. Her husband's name was Bert Ralston and they made a great marriage out of their life. He was born and raised in Tuskegee, Alabama. They were married in Meridian, Mississippi, and lived their entire lives there. He went to work for the Dixie Stockyards and worked there, as it turned out, for 12 years.

Like everyone else in the Ruff family, Uncle Bert had to start at the bottom and that included tractor driving. Grandfather Andrew bought his first gas powered tractor in the mid 1940s, a Farmall International Harvester. His son-in-law, Bert, would be one of the first to get time on that new machine. One thing you could say for sure, it would do more work in a day than eight mules. And that is the way new technology works. It makes the job quicker and easier and with better results. This change did not happen all at once though. At first it was about plowing and prepping the ground. Since there is more production, additional help is needed in other areas such as gathering and storage, not to mention maintaining the machinery. Also the sales of new tractors increased dramatic fashion, pulling more of the people to the metropolitan areas to build the tractors and many other gas powered machines. Tractors were just the beginning and almost at the same time mechanization of the harvesting and storage process began.

Joe always liked Uncle Bert and he made special plans to go out and watch Uncle Bert drive the new tractor. Sometimes Uncle Bert would even let Joe ride in his lap while he was plowing. One day when Joe was not there, Uncle Bert was on a particularly steep hill and the tractor turned over but to his good fortune, he jumped clear of the tractor. You see, older tractors like that one had two small front wheels that were very close together which made it much easier to overturn on unlevel ground. Later models would be corrected for this hazard by widening the space between the front wheels, so that they had less tendency to turn over.

Uncle Bert was an easy going guy, which didn't fit well into the Ruff mold, other than Uncle Ralph. Uncle Bert worked hard but without all the cursing and hell raising characteristics of his younger brother, Bubba. Even though Joe had ridden on the tractor many times with Uncle Bert, he was not there the day Uncle Bert turned the tractor over.

After about 12 years of putting up with Bubba , Uncle Bert and Aunt penny had had about enough. Bubba just knew one way and that was screaming and cursing all the time. No one who worked at the Stockyard wanted anything to do with him, except they had no choice since he was the General Manager. Their sole recourse was to tattle to the elder Andrew Ruff.

Katherine Ruff

Pop Andrew had one more daughter, born in 1925.

There was a forth child born to the Andrew Ruff family in the year 1925. It was a girl, and her name was Katherine. Joe didn't know her well as she left home at an early age.

Katherine was much more reserved than her older sister, more the quiet but good natured, very sweet person. Her hair was more of a dishwater blonde. Like most of the Carneys she was on the tall and thin side, when grown she was about 5 feet 7 inches tall with blue eyes, where Penny was about the same height but with black hair and coal black eyes. Both were slender in build. When Kathryn graduated High School she elected to attend the University of Texas where she received her degree in business administration. Following graduation she went to work for Delta Airlines as a Stewardess. Then she married a hometown boyfriend, Newton Borland. They had 4 children, 3 girls and one boy. They married during the last part of WW2. After an honorable discharge from the US Army the family moved back to Meridian for a short stint and then moved to Mobile, Alabama, where they lived and worked for about 8 years. Then they moved to Indiana which they would call home for the next 15 years or so. One of the three daughters would die from cancer. The oldest daughter would remain at the old homestead in Indiana. The youngest daughter would move to Phoenix, Arizona, and the one son would move to Birmingham, Alabama, and open and run a window business. The elder Newton Borland would move back to Meridian just before his death in 2008.

STOCKYARD HISTORY

AT THAT TIME, THE LOCAL draft board was going to draft Joe's Dad, but Pop Ruff went to the Board and told them that he could not run his Sale Barn business without him, so the draft deferred his Dad as necessary farm labor. Pop Andrew had sent both of them, Joe's Dad and his Uncle Ralph, to auctioneer school before the war started. Joe's Dad would go on to become a professional cattle auctioneer in addition to his other accomplishments. He was a great auctioneer, but on more than one occasion he lost an auctioneer's job because of his short temper, or 'it's my way or the highway' attitude but a great auctioneer none the less. And it paid well at the time and was a good way to make steady grocery money. On Dad's behalf though, buyers can be jerks at times. But it all goes with the territory, and the customer or buyer is, as a rule, the boss.

There was another local cattle slaughter house, Betzebees, which was located about 1/4 mile down the road from the Dixie Livestock Auction barn. The Stock barn owned what was in those days called a bobtail truck which was much smaller than what is now called a semi or 18-wheeler. It was a single axle truck. The bobtail truck was used to make local deliveries of maybe 8-10 cattle in one load. The truck had to cross what was known as Sowashee Creek on the way to the slaughter house. The creek bed was about 20 feet below the level of the road. It had been built that way on purpose in case flood waters might get over road. On one particular evening, flood waters were not a problem and the creek was low. When the truck reached the middle of the bridge, which was about 40 feet long, the bridge collapsed with the whole load of 10 cattle falling into the creek, backend first. Miraculously, none of the cattle or the driver were injured. All they had to do was round up and herd the cattle right on into the slaughter house.

There was always something exciting going on around the stock barn. On occasion a bull or a steer would jump the fences and get out across the railroad tracks and into downtown Meridian. When that happened, it always triggered the cowboys into action, including Bubba Ruff and one or two of his most trusted assistants. The horses used for rounding up cattle were housed at the stock barn and had their own large, private pen. Bubba and one or two of his assistants would saddle up and ride uptown and lasso the animal and drag it back to the stock barn. You might ask, why was this stock barn located so close to the downtown. It was because the stock barn was there long before most of the downtown was there. It's the same principal as the airports that are located too close to cities. The truth is that the airports were there first and then the town grew up around them.

The stock barn had for years done the 4H Club's annual Fat Calf Sale for them. After years of doing the sale, one year the Dixie Stockyard decided to donate the commissions made on the sale to the 4H Club. Of course these calves had been fed out to prime condition so they brought much more money than average cattle. And wouldn't you know that favor to the 4H Club caused the cattle ranchers to call a meeting and establish what is known as a Co-op Sales Barn of their own. Now in case you don't know what a Co-op Stockyard is, it is a Stock Barn where a lot of small shareholders each own a small number of shares. But then these shareholders feel obligated to sell their cattle at the Co-op Stock Sales Barn because they own a very small part of the business, never mind how small their fraction of ownership. This is by definition how socialism works.

Now since the stock barn had the investors' money, they didn't have to make a profit! Of course if you know anything or care about business at all, you know that businesses must make a reasonable profit or they must close their doors. So the first thing the so-called Meridian Livestock Auction did after it opened was start a Commission War. The Dixie Stockyards then played the cut commission war game until there wasn't any profit left. But a Co-Op Stockyard doesn't have to make a profit, and of course, it becomes a typical bureaucratic organization where anyone can just pass the buck to someone else. In addition, they just tell their shareholders that there was no profit that year. "But we sold your cattle cheaper than you could have sold them elsewhere!" You see, there is a head of this department and a head of that department, so that if you have a complaint you can't get to the one who's responsible. At a private operation the complaint goes straight to the owner.

But a funny thing happened. The Ruff brothers saw this thing coming and started an order buying business, that is, shipping cattle to feed lots in the western US. This was made feasible by the fact that there were not enough cattle in the West to fill the feed lots. The business of a feed lot is to fatten up the cattle for sale to slaughter houses. You see, the Southeastern part of the country was always the grazing center because there was more rain and a longer grazing season and believe it or not Texas does not have the most cattle. Florida does. The trick was also that the Ruff brothers had the experience and know how to buy the cattle that were worth the money. So Bubba Ruff, since he was better at buying cattle than dealing with people, and a few other buyers stayed on the road buying the cattle, and Uncle Ralph stayed with the home base and sold the cattle over the telephone. Their order buying business continued and flourished.

But, it wasn't too long before competition came to the order buying business as well. No hard feelings were felt because competition is fundamental in free enterprise; so long as its not a CO-OP, whose main design is to drive private enterprise out of business. And it came in the form of a young veterinarian who had , in the past, done a lot of work and gotten his start by doing veterinary work for the Dixie Stockyard. He opened up his own order buying business. But for one reason or another he went busted. Some say it was because his son, who was running the business for him, started gambling with the futures market; and others say it was just generalized poor management. Either way, you have to buy the cattle at the right price and then you have to have a reliable source that will pay for the cattle, but you also have to deliver consistency in price and quality. And to do this you have to have some skin in the game.

An odd thing happened later, after the Dixie had closed the Livestock auction part of the business. The City of Meridian decided to build two new overpasses across the railroad tracks. One of the overpasses would go right through the stockyard loading chutes. The city had the right to take the property but the law required them to pay the Ruff brothers a fair price. This was done through a law known as "Imminent Domain", wherein the city may take your land to build a Civil Structure for use by all the people, such as a school or government structure. This statute has been abused in recent decades by the US Supreme Court allowing Cities to take land away from private owners in order to allow them to sell it to commercial developers. And one of the most recent retired US Supreme Court Justices was allowed to do just that. This law was never intended for that purpose. That's a violation of the law!

So the Ruff brothers moved to the southwest side of the city about 5 miles out and built another barn. But this time it was a holding facility. They built a holding barn with plenty of outside roaming area and plenty of holding pens and a set of scales, and a separate office, with a bathroom, kitchen, a front foyer and four sales offices. This took the business up to the Reagan era. *And now we need to back up to the Depression Era.*

Chapter 3

Pop Andrew Ruff

JOE ALWAYS LOVED GOING to visit his Grandfather Ruff because he felt secure with his grandparents and there was no judgement of his actions. They were kind enough to allow him to stay for as much as a week and during those times, Grandfather Ruff would usually take him on a fox hunt.

Pop Andrew did buy another new tractor in the late 1940's and continued to lessen the number of mules that were needed on the farm. Up to this time he always had about eight to ten mules to do all the heavy plowing and clearing work on the farm. In addition to that, he had about 80 milk cows and about a dozen Fox Hounds. But more about the hounds later. So, when he bought the new tractor he also hired a colored man to drive it. His name was Isaac Sulligent. Each morning about daylight Isaac would come on the front porch of the house and tap on Pop Andrew's bedroom window to get his instructions for the day. Pop was a late sleeper during his middle to late years because he stayed up late at night reading history and politics and his fox hunting paper.

Isaac loved that tractor and he would drive it everywhere. He lived in one of grandfather Ruff's tenant houses and there was no rent. Grandfather Ruff allowed Isaac to use the tractor to go get groceries and for his personal transportation to and from town, which was about three miles away. This of course was in the 1940s. For certain, you couldn't do that today! The new tractor was also used when Isaac wanted to make the Honkey Tonks on Saturday and Sunday. And Isaac would take his wife, Honey, with him when he went to town. She would either ride on the bush hog or in his lap. It was sad, but one Sunday morning Isaac had gone to one of the local Honky Tonks and during a heated debate with another man, the other man stabbed him with a screw driver in the temple area just behind the left eye and killed him on the spot.

The new tractor even had a belt pulley that would pull a belt, which would power the silage machine that ground the corn and the stalks into silage to feed the mules and cows. But there was a problem. When the silage was blown into the silo, someone still had to walk on the top of it, packing the silage so the silo would hold more. This was the food for the dairy cows in the winter and a full packed silo would hold enough silage to last the 80 milk cows for the winter. In addition, he would plant oats in the fall for the dairy cows to graze on by January until the native clover and grass would begin to come on in March.

From the middle to the end of the 1940s would mark the beginning of the end for mule power. After about 1950 there would no longer be a separate pen at the front of the Dixie Stockyards for work mules. With the advent of the Ford tractor in the late 1940s almost all farmers would be able to afford some kind of a tractor. And a few years later garden tractors would make their appearance, making sure the mechanized stage was fast upon them. But with the elimination of many manual labor jobs came factory jobs of all descriptions. Once that happened, of course, the flight to the cities and the malls and the Metro areas began in earnest. By the 1950s most everyone lived in town or in the suburbs near the shopping.

Up until about the 1880s 75% of the American people lived in rural areas, but with the advent of automobiles and oil powered farm equipment the whole calculus changed. By the 1950s most people had moved to the metropolitan areas with less than 10% of the American people still living on farms and this number has continued to decline to about four percent today.

Chapter 4

Fox Hunting

GRANDFATHER ANDREW was an avid fox hunter. He had a pen of about a dozen fox hounds ready to hunt fox as soon as the work day was over. Pop Andrew was sometimes called Bud Ruff by his friends and business people he knew. He would build a den for the fox and would buy the best and largest red fox he could find. Now the first thing you need to understand is that in those days there were no red fox in Mississippi, only gray fox, and they were about half the size of a good red fox. Pop Ruff bought only the best, largest red fox that could be had. He special ordered them and the main key was that they had to be shipped by air in order to have the best chance of the fox being healthy enough to survive the trip and then being turned loose in the Mississippi wild. Pop ordered his large red fox by mail. They came in a crate and he would put the crate up snug against the entry to the den and thus allow the fox to escape the box into the den . Then he would leave them alone for a few weeks until they had time to acclimate and adjust to their new environment.

Joe was with his grandfather when he built the fox den. He frequently took Joe with him after the death of Joe's brother Brick. He likely thought little Joe needed more companionship after his brother's passing. Anyway the den was built underground and consisted of a large metal box for the den part, maybe three feet by two feet with a six or eight inch diameter concrete pipe leading into the den about eighteen inches in length. All of this was covered by about two feet of dirt to make it secure from dogs and any other predators.

Joe also remembered that Pop Ruff had a subscription to the Fox Hunting Newspaper which he read from cover to cover each month. Joe thought Pop Ruff loved fox hunting because it was fun to listen to the dogs chase the fox. And remember each dog had his particular bark sound so that you knew which dog or dogs were hot on the scent and which were not. Also the redeeming principle behind the whole hunt was that no one got hurt, the fox or the dogs. Once the fox went up a tree because the dogs were too close, the hunt was over and eventually the dogs would return to their pen, and the fox would return to his den. The hunt was usually a once a week activity, weather permitting.

It was always fun when Grandfather and three or four of his fox hunting friends would turn the fox hounds out of the pen just after dark and follow the hounds in their cars. They would listen to the hounds barking as they picked up the fox scent, and they could tell by the dogs' bark which dogs were on the trail of the fox. And finally after an hour or two, the dogs would tree the fox or loose their scent. The hunters would then walk into the area and find, with the flashlight, that the fox had indeed gone up a tree or been lost to the dogs altogether. The hunt might last from an hour to two hours then the hunt was over, and everyone went home. Sometimes the hunter friends would bring a fox hound of their own, so it was a friendly competition among the hunters as to whose dog treed the fox.

Now one must keep in mind that fox hunting can be done by horseback, but these men were all over fifty years old and were thus past that stage in life where they wanted to hunt by horseback. Surely you have seen the pictures of the British hunting fox with the horses jumping hedges and all dressed in white riding pants, red coats, and black hats. But that was then and this was just another way of hunting fox.

Now as for Joe, he would go on the hunt with Pop Ruff but would usually get tired before the fox was treed, and he would lie down and go sound asleep on the seat of granddad's car. And please remember, you must understand that the object of the fox hunt was not to kill the fox but to run him up a tree and then the hunt was over!!! That way, nobody got hurt. Least of all the fox. Pop Ruff didn't want those fox hounds to kill his red fox!

And what did those fox hounds eat? They ate the best corn bread that Momice Ruff could make daily and plenty of milk from the dairy. The balance of the corn bread was given to the farm hands who worked for Pop Ruff. In those days, nothing was wasted.

Chapter 5

The FED

BEING AROUND HIS ELDERS was a treat for Joe because he learned a great deal about the world and the politics connected to it. He committed many stories to memory and they began to shape his thoughts for the future. To explain a little about this, we listen to the elder Andrew Ruff. People shopped at local stores and there was always a small grocery store within spitting distance. Everyone knew everyone. You could buy all the groceries and necessities that you could haul home for about two dollars. The problem was having the two dollars. Andrew said the problem with the lack of money was in the way the country's money had been handled from the beginning.

According to Ruff, Alexander Hamilton and his cronies from the beginning, in 1791, were loyal to the British Crown. They had set in operation a *privately owned* Federal Bank. It would seem reasonable that a *privately owned* bank would by nature be of advantage to the ones who owned it. And this did seem to be true since the people kept losing their money and finding the financial situation of their country becoming worse as the years went on. They always had money losses and no one could seem to straighten out the money trail. The people ended up with a financial debt mess not of their making. And there was much discontent among the American people about the way their National banking was being handled.

So when President Andrew Jackson came on the scene in the early 1830s, he vowed to stop the financial blood loss by allowing the charter to expire on the *privately owned* Federal Bank. He said the banks were stealing from the people. There had been no *privately owned* Federal Bank since President Andrew Jackson had allowed its Charter to expire on purpose in about 1835. He saw the *privately owned* Federal Bank as a system to misappropriate and mishandle the peoples' money. This was done, and the government managed to function without a *privately owned* bank until 1913.

There are those who say, "Well, what about runs on the banks?" If the government isn't allowed to print money then there can't be a run on the banks. Government's only function should be to be see that there is adequate money in circulation. And if banks break the rules then they should be put out of business or sold. In other words, if a bank can't or won't play by the rules as set by the people, close them down and make room for a new bank owner.

Same thing applies with the banks and housing. If the banks over loan and shoot craps with the depositors' money, they should be shut down and bankers should go to jail just like anyone else does for taking the peoples' deposited money and shooting craps with it. And that is exactly what derivatives are. They are craps.

Now move forward to about the turn of the century, around 1900. The country had some anxious times over the years from 1835 to 1900, but in the process it became the greatest economic power in the world up to that time. Local and foreign bankers alike were desperate and scheming to wrestle control of the US economy through banking.

In 1910, a cabal of six men organized a secret meeting on Jekyll Island off the coast of Georgia. The meeting group contained two bankers and four politicians who would work towards and formulate a plan for the private takeover of the finances of the US government. It would take three years of work to implement the plan. Meantime, when elected, Woodrow Wilson would be their man to implement this plan. Wilson would be elected in 1912 and it would take less than a year to take over the important financial power reins of the American government. Their sinister plan was the smoothest plan ever devised by man .

On December 23rd, 1913 at 11:30 pm when most of Congress had already left for the Christmas holidays, they and Woodrow Wilson, the President, passed the law for the formation of the FED as we know it today, which is a privately owned bank about which no one knows of its ownership. They also passed the Individual Income Tax Law. And, as FDR would say, "That day will live in infamy." For at that very moment the American people lost control of their financial destiny.

Chapter 6

The Ruff Family Legacy

THE RUFF FAMILY HAD a reputation of being honest and hard working farmers though, and they seemed to be able to make ends meet even if sometimes it felt as if they might not make it. The elder Ruff, Andrew, had come to the area with his father, Gabriel, or Gabe for short, in just a wagon with his wife and five children in 1890. Andrew, was the second child and then there was one older sister, one younger brother and two younger sisters. Gabriel was a trader and of an entrepreneurial character and he soon began to accumulate land and equipment with which to farm.

In the early twenties many people sold their farms and moved to the cities where there were easier and more lucrative jobs to be had. And Gabriel bought their land as they left for the cities. Pretty soon he had accumulated hundreds of acres of land that he cleared and began farming

As Andrew, the oldest son, came along, he also was successful, and like his father, he was a good money manager and accumulated money and land and was likewise a hard, smart worker. He was a self educated man who read voracious amounts of material and loved history and in particular political history. Although he had little formal education, he educated himself by reading many books late into the night.

As we said before, in those days farming was all about horse power or maybe one should say mule power. Mechanical tractors were just beginning to come into the midwestern US, but the South was too poor to have them even if they were available. So mule power was a way of life in the rural south. Grandfather Andrew knew history well. He said that the Civil War had left the South destitute, but the twelve year occupation by the northern soldiers made most everyone in the South poor and almost destitute.

So Joe Ruff, Andrew's oldest grandchild, grew up very poor. The house in which Joe lived was a four room tenant house with two rooms that could be used as bedrooms and one with a fireplace that might be called a living room and one room that was the kitchen. There was cold water to the kitchen and no inside bathroom. They had what was called a slop jar which was your inside bathroom if you needed to use the bathroom at night. There was a wood stove in the kitchen for cooking and heat in the winter.

Now Joe and his big brother were two years apart in age but much farther apart in personality. The older brother, Brick, was big and strong for his age and very outgoing and adventuresome. He was always quick to take care of his little brother Joe though. Joe, on the other hand, was scrawny, small and skinny. He was intolerant of cow's milk and almost died of malnutrition before they discovered he could drink and tolerate goats' milk just fine. He also had a rectum that would sometimes prolapse and have to be pushed back inside manually, but this problem seemed to mend itself with age. He was also prone to colds, bronchitis, and pneumonia and had whooping cough at an early age. In addition, he would need to have his tonsils removed at age four.

Little Joe remembered that T&A like it was yesterday for the rest of his life. You have never seen a little guy fight so hard not to be put to sleep with that ether. It smelled awful and four year old Joe fought them off like he was fighting for his life. The surgery was done at the old St. Joseph's Hospital on 29th Avenue in Meridian. There were four grown people, including his parents, one on each extremity, trying to hold Joe down, and they still could not get the mask over his nose so that the ether could be administered. After much fighting, the nurse anesthetist talked with Joe in a soft, whispering tone and told him that if he would just allow her to lay the mask across his nose nothing would happen. Joe with great reluctance said alright. She gently laid the mask across his face, and the last thing he remembered was screaming. When he woke up his tonsils and adenoids had been removed.

His older brother was very protective of Joe. There was one instance when Joe was three years old and Brick was five, in which the neighbor boys were attempting to bully Joe. Brick was quick to rescue his little brother. He rushed in and punched both boys out and sent them home crying to their mother. Joe adored his big brother, Brick.

Joe's father, Bubba, saved enough money to buy an old model T Ford. In those days no one had lawn mowers so the weeds grew high in the yard. One day while his Mom had gone to the store, Brick decided to hide in the weeds of the front yard and surprise her when she returned. His Mom did not see him hiding in the weeds and ran across him as she pulled into the yard. The wheel of the car rolled across his abdomen and right away it was obvious that he was seriously injured. They quickly rushed him to the hospital where he was evaluated and admitted for observation. In those days, 1937, there were no doctors who did surgery of the abdomen in their small town. After a few hours of observation it was obvious that his injury might be terminal. In just twenty-four hours little Brick died from what was said to be a lacerated liver.

Joe's paternal grandparents lived a hundred yards up the blacktop paved road. Granddad Andrew, or Popeye, as Joe called him had built a monument of a two story home in 1918 which had three bedrooms and a bath up stairs and two bedrooms, a large formal living room, a large dining room and a kitchen with a stove that burned coal or wood. It was an elegant southern home with large columns on the front porch, a fit place to raise two boys and two girls. The elder Andrew would later build a real doll house in the front yard for the girls when they came along. And there was a large swing on that front porch where the family spent many a happy hour just relaxing.

Joe's Dad was the oldest child and Joe became the oldest grandchild with the passing of his five year old brother. The funeral for Brick was at Grandfather Andrew's home in the living room where the casket was placed on the right hand side of the room next to the windows which faced east. All the family and friends gathered on the front porch, foyer and living room for the funeral. Little Brick was buried in Magnolia Cemetery near where his great Grandfather Gabriel was buried.

Of course his Mother would never fully recover from the emotional trauma of that event and the extreme guilt she felt. And little Joe, age three, saw his Dad cry for the first time.

It was terribly lonely and shocking for Joe at age three to see his five year old brother, defender and playmate, lying in that casket. It was a life changing event for the whole family. But little Joe had lost his playmate forever. The funeral was a standing room only affair and Joe remembered for the rest of his life that sweet expression on Brick's face as he lay there motionless in his casket. Little Joe had to be raised up to be able to view his brother's body in the casket, but little Joe was too young at the time to grip the reality of what was going on.

Fate works in strange ways at times. The very next year Big Mama, the elder Andrew's mother, passed and there little Joe was again, viewing her body in a much larger casket in his Grandparents' living room. So Joe learned at an early age that death is a very real thing that comes to visit all of us at some point in our lives. He didn't understand why, but by now he knew that everyone would at some point be visited by what some might call the grim reaper...

Chapter 7

Momice Ruff and Cotton Pickin'

BIG MAMA RUFF OCCUPIED one of the three upstairs bedrooms and the two daughters of Andrew and Momice occupied the other two. Joe could still remember meeting Big Mama, and she was a real talker. He remembered her saying that "everyone has a living and a killing coming and they're gonna get em both." Of course the meaning was that everyone has one life to live and they were also going to die. So live it any way you want, but you are not getting out of this world alive. Never been a truer statement.

Momice Ruff was from a prominent family, the Curwells, who lived on the southwest corner of Meridian town ship also known as Lost Gap. The Curwell family had a long history of patriotism to the United States, as one of the Curwell men had been a Colonel in Washington's Revolutionary Army. In those days it was both common and proper for young ladies to be married at a young age. Momice Ruff was fifteen and Joe's Grandfather Andrew was twenty-three when they married. This would have been in about 1913.

After his brother Brick's death, life had a distinct void for little Joe who had lost more than a brother. Brick was his playmate and guardian. Without Brick, little Joe became very unsure about the world that was left to him and his self confidence suffered a blow that no one else was aware of.

One Sunday morning Joe had been dressed for Church early and while waiting for his mother to take him to church. His parents didn't go to church, they just dropped him off. While waiting, he ventured across the road into the cow pasture where there was a small stream. This was the pasture that his grandfather used as grazing for the dairy cows. Without realizing it, he got his new church shoes and Sunday clothes all muddy. When he got back to the house it was not the warmest of welcomes that he got from his mother.

There was other excitement for Joe. Grandfather Ruff always planted the hill across from the house in cotton. This forty acre hill was called Aunt Nett's Hill because it was left by Gabriel Hawkins Ruff, in his will, to the youngest of his five children, Nett. She had then sold that plot to Joe's grandfather, her older brother, Andrew, or Popeye, as we now know him.

The colored people who picked the cotton would put the cotton in long bags that they drug along with them. The bag would hook over their head with a strap and drag along beside them and when filled with cotton it was very, very heavy. When and only when the bag was full, they would dump the bags into a large wagon which the mules would then pull up to the barn when the wagon was full. Joe would never forget how those colored folks looked out for him when he came into the field where they were picking. They were all about letting him help them with the cotton picking but always watching to be sure he didn't get hurt. They even got him a small bag to help them with the cotton picking and would let him pick his own row of cotton. Of course one of them would always come along behind him and pick the cotton he missed. Remember, he was only four at the time.

Far from what many people thought, the white and colored people got along well in their community and looked out for each other no matter what color they were. Joe couldn't speak for other communities, but in their community the races were very close and if there was friction between them, Joe couldn't tell it. Joe only saw his grandfather show any violence toward a colored person on one occasion, and we will talk about that later on.

Also Joe remembered that his Grandfather Ruff always wore a brown business suit with a white shirt and tie even if he was helping the colored guys with an outside job. The 1930s were a special time in the Ole South. Many of the factories in the North had closed their doors when the Great Depression started in 1930. So many of the colored people who had moved North in the 1920s came back home to the South when the factories closed down. They were in need of work, any kind of work, to put food on the table, and there was plenty of work, more than enough. Many a morning after Joe had spent the night at his grandparents house, he would walk out on the back porch at daylight with his grandfather, and there would be ten to fifteen young healthy colored men standing there in the back yard wanting to work. Pop would work as many as he could and send the rest home. They all brought their lunch with them in a gallon metal molasses can and they always brought corn bread submerged in molasses with a big slice of ham or some bacon in it. If you had that for your noon meal you could make the day. Also for some of them who didn't have food Joe's grandmother would feed them on the porch out back of the kitchen. She always made plenty of vegetables, cornbread and ham or bacon.

Now remember, Joe's grandfather had 8-10 mules and harnesses for all of them so there was always work for 8-10 men. Grandfather Ruff also had a dairy where he milked about 80 cows. When homogenized milk came in he did that too. Pop had a delivery truck that took milk to the city every morn-ing to various restaurants. The delivery man was named Baker Armstrong and Joe always loved going with him to deliver the milk. He always left at 4 am sharp. He had really bad asthma though and eventually moved to Southern Arizona where the climate was better for his asthmatic condition.

Joe could only recall one incident in about 1938 when he was four years old that his grandfather was involved in what could be called racial, but with Grandfather it was all about respect. Grandfather was building a fence corner near Joe's house. He had taken off his brown dress coat and had the sleeves of his white shirt rolled up. He had three or four colored boys helping build that fence corner. There was one that was about fifteen years old who kept sassing and arguing every time Pop would tell them to do this or that. Final-ly, Pop grabbed a hoe and struck him across the head, knocking him to the ground. He then stomped him in the face twice and told him to get up, leave and don't come back....end of story. He didn't come back!

The family was concerned that since Joe's older brother was gone that Joe needed a playmate. His grandmother, Momice Ruff, had a colored maid and housekeeper whose name was Claud. Claud had a grandson who was Joe's age about four. It was decided that Claud would bring her grandson each day and drop him at Joe's house as she walked to work. Claud only lived about half a mile from Joe's grandmother's house, making it convenient to leave him on the walk to work. His name was Robert Lee and Joe and Robert Lee hit it off great. They mostly played outside in the dirt where they made toy tractors and cars and trucks from thread spools and tin cans and rubber bands. The toys they made were primitive but there was no money to buy real toys for anyone. They had wonderful times together and became great friends. It never occurred to either of them that they were not the same color. They were just friends. However, after Joe moved to the city, he would never see Robert Lee again. Their lives just went in different directions.

Chapter 8

Early Schooling

WHEN JOE TURNED SIX years old in April of 1940, his parents decided that he should attend school in the City of Meridian rather than the county rural school nearest their home. They enrolled him in Stevenson Elementary, one of six elementary schools in the city.

As if little Joe hadn't already had enough trauma in his early life, his mother went to the most expensive clothing store in town and bought him knickers to wear to school, and he also had to wear dress shoes. You see his parents over killed on everything because of the extreme guilt feelings they had about his brother Brick's death, especially Joe's mother. All this to make him dress for school as though he was going to church. This is exactly what little Joe didn't need. He didn't need to feel different or special from the other little boys in his school. He just wanted to feel like a normal six year old first grader. But dressing this way had precisely the opposite effect. All of the other little guys in the 1st grade were wearing blue jeans and tennis shoes. And to make it worse the other kids chided him about his clothes, which made him feel even more afraid and inferior. This all started what came out to be a disastrous first grade year for Joe.

Most of the kids would get to school about 8 am and play tag and run a lot before the bell rang for school to start. They played a game of tag with a tree being safe and if you ran from the tree others would chase and try to tag you before you could get back to the tree. Joe found that he was a fast runner and rarely could anyone catch him. This would become more apparent with age.

Ms. Brewster was the principal and she would ring the hand held bell at 8:30 am sharp. The students would then all gather in front of the school and stand in line according to grade, all 1st graders together, 2nd graders, etc. The stairs to the building were about fifteen steps high leading into a large two story brick building through two huge doors. The entry to that school was intimidating all by itself. It housed grades one through six, each grade having its own separate room. 1st grade was just inside the door and to the left.

Ms. Brewster, standing on the top of the steps, would see that every child was properly lined up, and then she would make any special announcements that needed to be made. This was followed by the Pledge of Allegiance to the flag of the United States, and then she or one of the teachers would give a prayer after which all of the students would proceed to their classrooms. There were scrap metal bins at all the schools and even though the United States was not officially at war with Japan you would think that they were very much on a war footing. But, except for listening to the older folks talk, it was operation normal for the kids.

The class room was a whole 'nother trauma experience. Joe's 1st grade teacher was a very young and new to teaching flaming red headed disciplinarian name Miss Moore. She saw right away that Joe had problems sitting still so she put him in the middle of the front row. And Joe really could not sit still. He either blurted out answers or he was quiet and shy. There seemed to be no middle ground. All he could think of was recess and getting out to run and play. He was totally intimidated by the whole school experience. Here was a little six year old whose whole life thus far had been spent on his grandfather's farm with few friends and all of a sudden he's put into a totally disciplined situation. It was a totally disastrous year for Joe with constant hand paddling's, visits to the cloak room and also the Principals office. He was branded a bad child who would not follow instructions or do the work.

What a sad thing to be branded a BAD CHILD, rather than a child who had a textbook case of ADHD (attention deficit hyperactivity disorder). But so it was in the year 1940...and at that time no one had even heard of ADHD.

Things went from bad to worse right away when Ms. Moore spanked his hands with the ruler. This became a daily ritual; the whipping of his hands with the ruler were punctuated by trips to the cloak room for isolation. His mother was called into the matter, and it was determined that Joe was just one of those bad kids who would not be still, sit down, behave and do the work. This went on the whole year, and all little Joe could think about was getting out for recess or going home. The situation never changed that whole year and Joe had whelps on his hands from the daily ruler spankings.

Finally, at the end of the year, there was a real problem of whether or not to pass him on to the 2nd grade. He didn't seem dumb, but he seemed to be caught up in a world of his own. His mind and attention were hardly ever focused on the class room task at hand. He just couldn't concentrate on the classroom work. HE WAS LABELED A BAD CHILD....

After much soul searching, it was decided to move him to a different school, Marion Park Elementary, where a dear friend of the Ruff family was teaching the 2nd grade. Her name was Ms. Josephine Garrett, and since she was a friend, she knew the Ruff family well. She was a blondish haired woman, slim and was really good at working with students like Joe. So little Joe was transferred to Marion Park Elementary School for the 2nd grade. He and Ms. Garrett hit it off well, and before long, she had him doing better in all phases except math. He did improve with the friendly tutelage of Ms. Garrett.

By now the Bubba Ruff family had a new baby girl and had moved to town. They were only four blocks away from the school, so Joe could walk to school. Joe had a hard time learning to read, but he did make slow progress with Ms. Garrett's kind attention. To Joe she was like having a private tutor. Joe's dad decided to help him with his math though by having teaching sessions with Joe at home in the evenings. First his Dad would explain addition and subtraction to him and then have Joe work a problem to see if he understood. If Joe could not repeat what his Dad had just shown him, his Dad would take his belt off and whip him and then repeat the same procedure until Joe could work the math problem. Sometimes it required multiple whippings before Joe could do the math problem. Dad would repeat the process and whip him again and again until Joe could do the problem. This went on weekly until Joe learned basic math. Joe finally learned the math but hated the whole process and school as well. Joe went on and finished the 2nd and 3rd grades at Marion Park Elementary school, after which his parents decided that he should return to Stevenson Elementary for the 4-6 grades. Joe never liked school after that and only longed for recess when in school and the summers when he did not have to attend school.

When the family moved to town, Dad and Mom bought a house on 25th Avenue where the family lived for the next several years. Joe quickly met a friend who lived three houses down the street. His name was Hugh Albertson, and they became fast friends. They were, as the saying goes, 'partners in crime', not literally, but close friends. There was another boy an only child that lived across a vacant lot from them whose name was Dickie Brown. He was in Joe's class at school. Dickie was a straight A student, and of course, he didn't like Hugh or Joe. It was really just a friendly rivalry though, nothing serious.

One day Hugh and Joe got into a rock throwing fight with Dickie and another one of their friends. The rock throwing went on for quite a while until either Hugh or Joe hit Dickie in the mouth with a rock and broke off one of his new permanent front teeth. Anyway Dickie's mother told Joe's parents that Joe started the rock fight in the first place and had damaged her son for life. Joe's parents asked Joe what happened and he told them that they were all throwing rocks and that Dickie got hit in the mouth and that he didn't know who threw the rock that broke the tooth. Joe's parents listened to Joe's account of what happened and then listened to Dickie's mother's accounting and of course they took her side and Joe got a beating by his Dad over that. The theme was always the same, Joe was wrong and his Dad was not going to tolerate Joe dragging the family name through the dirt.

The only thing Joe learned from this that if caught in a dispute with anyone his parents would always listen to both sides and no matter the situation, they always came down on the side against Joe. This taught him early in life that there was no one that he could trust to be on his side, not even his own mother or father. Not a good place for a now 7 year old. It seemed to Joe that in any conflict his parents would always find a way to blame him. Anything gone errant, Joe was to blame. And would you believe that Joe and Dickie went all the way through high school together, playing in the Band together, and Dickie never made eye contact with or spoke to Joe again?

While living on 25th Avenue, Joe remembers that on his 8th birthday he had a birthday party at his house and his mother had told him that he could invite a few of his classmates. He said okay, that was great, and he invited his whole class. And to make it worse they all showed up, all 30 of them. And wouldn't you know that there was a hard rain downpour that lasted the entire afternoon. Joe was lucky that there was a brand new basement under the house with a brand new hardwood floor just waiting for 30 eight year olds to play a game called get your shoes wet and see how far you can skid on those new hardwood floors. After the party it looked like 1000 cars had slammed on their brakes and left long black rubber marks. Joe's Mother was fit to be tied, but she kept her cool. They were able to get the black tennis shoe marks up later with a lot of scrubbing.

Joe was beginning to become fairly savvy by now that the world was not necessarily a friendly place or even a safe place. He was outside in the yard one evening just after dark when he saw two boys about 15 years old walking down the side walk on the other side of the street. He was outside because Dad was inside and he was afraid to be anywhere around his Dad. He tried to stay away from him. The two boys were arguing, about what he could not tell, but the conversation became more heated, and as they got much closer the larger of the two boys turned and punched the smaller boy in the face, and he fell to the ground. They were only 40 feet away, and when the smaller boy attempted to get up, the larger boy hit him again in the face. Joe could never stand to see anyone abused. He must have learned this from Brick. Joe was only eight, but before Joe even realized what he was doing he had run across the street and jumped on the back of the larger boy and began clawing at his face and beating him on the back of the head.

Before the larger boy, who was more than twice Joe's size, could react to Joe being on his back, Joe's father, hearing the commotion, came out of the house and came running towards the scene to break up the fight. Before he could get there, Joe fell to the ground, and the two boys fled the scene. Joe gave his Dad a full accounting of what had happened, and this time Joe wasn't found to be the guilty party.

In all fairness, Joe's Dad had lost the son who was most like him, and he was still grief-stricken. On the other hand, Joe was the scrawnier of the two boys and was nothing like his Dad, and his mother felt a real need to protect him from a father who was short on tolerance and quick to discipline with little provocation. His father was also insanely jealous of anyone that his mother felt affection or likeness for. This made Joe a ripe target for his Dad's anger any time that Dad was upset, which was most of the time.

The unfairness of that situation though was that Joe's mother would keep a mental list of the things that she felt Joe had done wrong in recent weeks or months and then relate the list to his Dad when she became angry at Joe. It was a kind of a blackmail list, most unfair, which created a triangular relationship between Joe and his parents. This was unfortunate because it made it so that again, Joe felt he could really trust no one. And that made for a world of isolation and fear for Joe; since it meant to him that there was really no one that he could ever trust completely, not even his own mother. All people and all children make mistakes and commit wrongs; and to be held hostage for those transgressions can only lead to increased anxiety and fear in a child.

Joe's Dad thought that children and farm animals were a lot alike. You just whip them into line with physical punishment, and they should do just fine until they make another mistake. Never mind that they don't understand why you are beating them. Fear of physical punishment should do the job. Once again, he always said he was not going to have his child drag the Ruff family name through the "dirt."

Now Joe's mother was a thinker, a very deep thinker. She really tried hard to figure out what the real meaning of life was. Joe would have to give her credit for that. As much as he would fault her for it later, she did begin to find the truth to life by the time she was about thirty-five. She always wanted to do the right thing for the right reason and Joe thought that in her religious search for answers she finally found Christian Science. Joe was about 13 or 14 when she made the switch.

Christen Science is and was based on the power of positive thinking. In other words, if you think negative thoughts, chances are things will turn bad for whatever situation you may be laboring over at the time. On the other hand, if you keep your thoughts positive, things will turn out for better; as long as you are able to accept the solution as God's will in that situation. That part always seemed reasonable and made sense, but with the way Joe had been treated over his lifetime, it was SO HARD to let go and think positively. Joe would remain paranoid and suspicious of everything and everyone for a very long time. It would take him years to overcome at least part of this paranoia which had been drilled into him throughout his childhood years from trusting no one to at least trusting SOMEONE.

Chapter 9

Joe and Santa Claus

ONCE JOE FOUND OUT what he had to do to get a C- in school, he was able to progress from grade to grade as a 'tail end Charlie' even though he only liked recess and summers . It wasn't that Joe was dumb. His mind was just other places. He had a short attention span. Joe was a natural athlete though and was the fastest runner in his school. During recess the boys usually played softball. The boys would choose up sides and Joe was always chosen in the first round. He learned to catch a fly ball early and could hit the ball as well. He had excellent hand eye coordination. He would have loved school if the whole thing was like recess.

By the Christmas when Joe was 10 years old , 1944, Joe got a pair of football pants, a helmet, and shoulder pads for Christmas. By then he and his family had moved within the city to just one block away from the Meridian High School Football stadium. The first thing Joe did was don his new gear and walk up to the stadium and play football with his friends. He imagined in his own mind that he was one of the greats who had played in this stadium. What a time and what a day.

However, all was not well between Joe and Mama this Christmas because this was the first time Joe had challenged Mama on the existence of Santa Claus. My goodness, Joe was 10 years old, and all his friends were kidding him about his insistence that there really was a Santa at the North Pole who hooked up those reindeer and flew through the heavens to visit all the little children of the world. And this was not to mention that Mama had taken him into one of the department stores two weeks before Christmas and looked at a pair of red football pants just like the ones that Santa brought.

How stupid did Mama think Joe was? Why was Mama just living in her own world of fantasy? "Oh yeah, and I still believed in the tooth fairy, right?", Joe thought. Joe's Mother was literally crushed that at age 10 he didn't believe in Santa Claus any more. She was actually angry. Now how long did she think he should continue to believe, when all his friends were kidding him about it, not to mention that Santa Claus in the physical sense was impossible? I mean how could that fat old guy get down any chimney, let alone ours? Well, this created an emotional stress bomb for his mother. But she finally got over it.

Now another child was born to the parents, a boy. They named him Andrew the III. Now they already had a 3rd, that was the first child, Brick. This was a very conscious effort to forget the first child, who died from his injuries after having been run over by his mother, ever existed. He should have been named the IV, but Mama insisted on pretending that Brick had never lived. Her feelings here were certainly understandable; but they were also pathological.

Chapter 10

World War II

THOUGH JOE WAS A CHILD during WW2, it was the last war that the American people would be 100% vested in. That is, "We are all in this together; now let's kick ass!" The United States had scrap metal bins at all the schools and the people used much of their money to buy war bonds. By and large the Americans believed in their government and fully supported the war effort. All Joe could think about was that he wanted to be a P-40 pilot and later when the P-51 came out he wanted to fly those too.

EVERY SATURDAY HIS mother would give him twenty five cents, a quarter, and he would go to the movie and stay all day. There was always a rooster that came out and crowed followed by a news reel on the war. That was the highlight of the day for Joe because sometimes they showed actual war films of fighter planes, and of course, it was always 'us good guys against the bad guys, the Germans or the Japanese'. Joe wanted to fly one of those fighter planes. Then there was a cartoon made by Disney and then the main feature, which could be the Lone Ranger and Tonto, Roy Rogers or Gene Autry. It cost 10 cents to get in the movie, and that left 15 cents to spend on candy and popcorn, and that was plenty because candy bars were 5 cents and so was popcorn. It was an all day affair in his little city. All the kids looked forward to Saturdays.

Another thing Joe remembered was that whatever the news media said, that was the absolute truth, and the people never questioned what they said. And in the late 1930s the family would all join around the family's big beautiful RCA Victor or Philco radio and listen to the fireside chats of President Roosevelt.

Chapter 11

The Ruff Family and Politics

ON SUNDAY EVENINGS Joe and his family used to listen to the radio and Joe learned a great deal about politics and world affairs and what HIS family thought about it all. Grandfather Andrew Ruff was concerned about the direction that politics was turning in the US and he gave the following account. There was much to question about what some thought to be President Roosevelt's socialistic approach to the solution of the financial problems in which the country found itself embroiled. Some also believed that he purposely provoked Japan into attacking Pearl Harbor in order to get the US into a war with Japan and that this provocation had to do with control of the Pacific rim countries and trade with them. Also, some say that Roosevelt and his Secretary of State, George Marshall, knew the day before the Pearl Harbor attack that two Japanese carriers were sitting 200 miles off the Hawaii Coast and what other reason would they be there for if not to attack Pearl Harbor?

This was Dec 6, 1941. Hind sight is 100%. As Mr. Roosevelt had said on December 8th, 1941, December 7th , 1941 would be a day that would " live in infamy." More than 2400 American soldiers, sailors and airman would lose their lives at Pearl Harbor on that day and to think that anyone had known about the attack on the day before was simply unthinkable.

On December 8th, 1941, President Roosevelt went before Congress and asked for a declaration of war on Japan which was granted, a Pacific war that would last nearly four years before Japan's unconditional surrender in Tokyo Bay in the late summer of 1945.

The Ruff family, especially the elder Andrew, who read about politics and history constantly, thought much of the monetary difficulties of the country had been caused by the government meddling in the finances of business where they had no expertise or business. Some blamed Herbert Hoover, but others said the horse was already out of the barn long before Hoover. The elder Ruff said the whole banking mess was caused by Woodrow Wilson and his cronies advocating and allowing the *Private banks* to take over our Federal Banking System.

Some said the formation of the FED bank and individual income tax were big problems created by Woodrow Wilson. The big problem with money and the government is that the government gets to put all manner of things on their wish list and then tax the people to get that money.

But many of the people had a different vision. They thought the country had done very well without a privately held Federal Bank so why change. But Woodrow Wilson and his group knew the only way to get the spending they wanted was to take the banking system away from the people and have it under private interest control.

The people's position, or many of them, was that America had functioned very well financially from the time of President Andrew Jackson, 'Old Hickory' as they called him, in the 1830s when he did away with the independently owned banking system created by Alexander Hamilton and his group who were loyal to the British Crown rather than the American people. In other words, America had no *Private* ownership of its banking system from 1935 until 1913 and got along fiscally well without a private ownership of the country's banking. So why did we need one in 1913?? President Jackson was vehemently opposed to independent bankers being in charge of the peoples' money. So he simply allowed the time for the banking charter to expire and refused to renew it.

Now there is even a gruesome account of exactly how a few individuals circumvented due process to get that legislation for the FED, as it is known today, passed.

Backing up one step further, Woodrow Wilson, who by way of being president of Princeton University, became, on a long shot, governor of New Jersey and then President of the United States. And taking one more step backwards, the Democrat party, of which he was the nominee, would never have won the Presidency in 1912 if Teddy Roosevelt had not formed a third party, the Bull Moose party, and thus split the Republican vote. Roosevelt was an arch rival and enemy of Taft, who was President from 1908 to 1912, and who had gone through the convention process and won the Republican nomination for President.

Woodrow Wilson was actually elected in the same manner as Bill Clinton when Ross Perot ran on a third party ticket and split the Republican vote, getting 19% of the popular vote. Otherwise The United States would never have had the Clintons in the White House. And this is not to mention that Bill Clinton got only 39% of the popular vote which made him a minority President. Some would call that a blessing and others would call it a curse. And don't forget, Woodrow Wilson gave us the predecessor to the United Nations and the League of Nations, which was supposed to be the 'end of all wars.' He was an imperialist of the first degree .

Chapter 12

Joe Ruff, Age 11-13

IN 1945 JOE'S DAD HAD the opportunity to buy a 200 acre farm just outside Meridian in the community of Marion. It was a small bedroom community only five miles from town and conveniently located to commute back and forth to town. So they moved back to the country, five miles out of town. At the time Joe didn't realize what this move actually meant for an 11 year old boy.

The first thing his Dad did was to fence in a large chicken yard and populate it with about two dozen laying hens. Taking care of the chickens was to be Joe's job and that included keeping the weeds cut. Then Dad hauled home not one but two milk cows, and they were also Joe's cows to milk twice a day, seven days a week. Cows also sometimes kick and more than a few times Joe got kicked off his stool and into the wall. Then Dad planted a large garden when spring came and Joe also had to keep the weeds out of that and water the garden. And finally, there was the large yard that had to be mowed. That was also Joe's job. All these tasks were tied to whether or not Joe was allowed to go play baseball and visit with his friends in the community.

No question, Joe had a rude awakening to what living on a farm was like, at least in the Ruff family. Dad felt that Joe's experience on the farm should be a rich one indeed like the one he had when he was a young boy. None of Joe's friends in the community had to do many tasks. They had more time to play. But Joe tried to make the best of the situation and do enough work that he could then go play with his friends.

Another thing Joe's Dad did was to buy a pony and a wagon for the kids. Joe thought that would be fun as well. There was only one small problem and that was that every time Joe took his little sister and brother for a pony ride in the wagon, the pony would break and run for the house when they got to Buck Barnett's grocery store, which was about 1/3 of a mile from the house. This happened several times before Joe mentioned what the pony was doing to his Dad. Dad scoffed at the idea that Joe couldn't manage that pony's bad behavior. Anyway, he said he would take a ride with Joe and his little sister, who was about six at the time. So Dad, little sister and Joe took off in the pony wagon towards Buck Barnett's store late one evening right about dark with Dad driving and Joe and his sister also in the wagon. It was after dark and off they went and just as they approached the store the pony made his break for the house. Joe knew this was going to happen, so when the pony started to break for the house Joe just stepped off the back of the wagon. Dad and little sister were still in the wagon, and when Dad pulled on the reins to stop the pony, the reins broke! By then the pony was up to full speed, which was about 15 miles per hour. Dad jumped out of the wagon with little sister in his arms, falling and injuring his shoulder and receiving a puncture wound to his elbow. Fortunately his little sister was not injured. In short, Dad made the pony and wagon go away.

THE COMMUNITY HAD A baseball team too that played in a cow pasture. They didn't have uniforms because no one could afford to buy them. They used old pieces of tarp for bases and most shared a glove that someone else owned. There was no specific age group. Boys as young as eight or as old as fifteen might be on the team. The Marion team played other communities and the games were always on Saturday afternoon. The local Methodist preacher was the coach of Joe's team. His name was Brother Tom.

One position that no one wanted to play was catcher and one of the reasons was that you needed a catcher's mitt and a protector for your chest and a catcher's mask. Joe was able to finagle to get the equipment and thus he became the catcher for the team even though he couldn't even throw the ball as far as 2nd base. But each year his arm grew stronger so that after two or three years he could 'smoke' that ball down to 2nd base.

AT THE TIME, THE CITY of Meridian had a class B professional baseball team. One of the older men in the community was the foul ball chaser for the Meridian Millers as they were named. Some of the kids could go with him to the games, and in return for chasing foul balls they got in free, and the team would give them a baseball. So that was how they got many of the balls that were used for their community team.

JOE MADE FRIENDS WITH the catcher of the pro team. His name was Danny Long. He was twenty-two years old and he was Joe's hero. Joe wanted to grow up to be a handsome specimen just like Danny. And Joe was constantly trying to fix Danny up with local women since he had no wife or girlfriend. It never worked though. Maybe Danny just couldn't find the right girl. Joe asked Danny why he was playing for a minor league team, not in an insulting way, just the way kids ask questions. Danny came right back with "Because I couldn't hit and I couldn't throw." As Art Linkletter would say, "Kids say the darndest things."

In grade six, all students attended May Day at Kate Griffin Jr. High School to familiarize them with the school they would be attending the next year. All six elementary schools descended on the junior high school on the same day to get a look at it. The junior high school was also interested in looking for potential athletes for the junior high school athletic programs. One of the events they had was a fifty yard dash to see who were the fastest runners and on the tryout there were about 25 runners who lined up for the 50 yard dash, Joe being one of them . At the finish line it was Woody Aarons, first, and Joe was second by about one foot, almost a photo finish. So it was determined that Joe was a real mover and shaker. But this was just prior to Joe's fractured ankle.

You see, an unfortunate accident happened about a month later that would forever end Joe's athletic aspirations. It had just rained and the grass was wet. Joe was ridding his bicycle in a neighbor's yard when he made a sharp turn, and he and the bike went down. His left foot got caught between the seat and the frame of the bike, and his ankle was slightly twisted. Joe's friend's mother ran out and without thinking grabbed the bike and jerked straight up. She was trying to help, but when she jerked up on the bike it broke Joe's ankle. When he got to the doctor's office, an x-ray revealed that he had a fracture of the fibula one-half inch from the distal end, and the bone was separated about three-sixteenths of an inch. Doctors back then didn't know that a fracture like that should have a screw put in it to reconnect the two pieces of bone. As a result, Joe had a lose ankle and he could never run like he had before ever again; in fact even walking caused it to swell. That ended Joe's athletic aspirations.

As though that wasn't enough, almost exactly a year later Joe was about a mile from the house riding a pony and made a sharp turn and the pony fell, pining Joe's left leg underneath between the pony and the ground. Would you believe this time it was a fracture of the tibia. That's the big bone of the leg between the ankle and the knee. Well, it was another ride to the hospital and this time it was a long leg cast from the ankle almost to the hip. Seems like Joe couldn't win for losing. This time his mother put Joe in the downstairs guest room so he wouldn't have to climb the stairs to his bedroom. Then when the cast came off, Joe would have to learn to walk all over again.

In the sixth grade, which was Joe's last year in elementary school, Joe had started playing the trumpet because he was always searching for new interests to learn about and conquer. So he turned his efforts toward music.

Chapter 13

Joe at Age 13

JOE STILL REMEMBERED when at 13 years of age he was given his first real job at the auction barn on sale day. He was the one who sat right beside the chute that led into the auction ring. The cattle all had ear tags that were clamped to their ears when they were first unloaded and came in through the receiving area. Joe's job was to look at the tag in the animals ear, write it's number on the sales ticket and place it on the window ledge to his right so that Uncle Bert, who sat next to the window and to the left of the Auctioneer, could get the ticket out of the window, fill out who bought the animal and the price, and then pass the ticket to the man who weighed the animal. It was quite a process to watch. Everyone had to do his part and make no mistakes in order to have no errors and keep the sale moving at a fast clip. If you had 800 head of cattle to sell, you must move at a pretty fast clip. The difficult part about Joe's job was that, in the case of smaller animals, two or three of them might sometimes be in the front exit chute at the same time and Joe would have to write down the numbers of all of them and be sure he put the proper ticket on the window for Uncle Bert. This sounds easy, but when the calves are pushing backwards and forwards in the chute and changing positions, it's easy to make a mistake and pass the wrong ticket. And of course this was always an opportune time for Bubba Ruff, Joe's Dad, who was always in the ring and yelling "Yes" every time a bidder nodded his head, would embarrass Joe with loud and ugly correction telling Joe how "You have to pay attention to what you're doing!", as if Joe didn't already know that. And of course, in front of a packed house this was humiliating in itself. It wasn't so much what he said but the obnoxious manner in which he did it.

After about 12 years of trying to fit in with the Ruff family, Uncle Bert and Aunt Penny would decide that they needed a change. Leaving Meridian though was out of the question because Aunt Penny was, again, her mother's closest friend and ally. They saw each other almost every day until the elder Momice Ruff passed away at 85 years of age. But it wasn't fair to Aunt Penny for her to be her mother's closest friend because it kept her from having very many friends her own age.

Uncle Bert and Aunt Penny decided to open a salvage business just down the street from the Livestock auction. Now they had a business of their own where they just had to answer to their customers. Their business, at first, was slow for sure. They built a regular clientele who would always come check to see if they had a product before going to buy things elsewhere. You could never tell what Uncle Bert and Aunt Penny might have. They might even have a jeweler's safe for sale. You just never knew. They would buy truck loads of stuff starting with toys on up and if you wanted to, you could even do your Christmas shopping there. Joe thought that if they had started sooner they could have been the next Walmart instead of Sam Walton. A lot of it is being at the right place at the right time. Also remember what Sam Walton said when he went through the first big market downer, "Well, it was all just paper when I started, and it's still all just paper."

Within this 100x75 foot building was a small office, about 8x8, in which there was room for just one person and a desk, and that was Aunt Penny's desk. She was the one who collected all the money and kept up with all the expenses and taxes, and this was the only air conditioned space in the building. One day the IRS showed up to audit the business. "Fine", said Aunt Penny, "But you can't use my office because I am using it, and the only place available for you is outside the building." One of them said, "What can we use for a desk?" She said, "I have two old school desks that I can put outside the front door of the building for you." One of them said, "That will be fine." Now this was in July and in Mississippi the temperature on a typical July day is about 98 degrees with high humidity. It took those two guys ten minutes to go through those papers and finish that audit!

Another thing about Uncle Bert is that he was a hunter-fisherman extraordinaire. He lost the sight in his right eye due to a virus at about age 20. He was able to switch to left handed shooting with no problem and could even kill a dove on the fly with a 22 caliber rifle. But he was a bass fisherman par excellence. Sometimes he would take Bubba Ruff with him and Uncle Bert would catch five fish for every one that Bubba caught. They would go before daylight many times. And Joe asked Uncle Bert if he wasn't afraid of being bitten by a water moccasin in the dark. He replied that he always wore a pair of rubber boots, knee high, and "If you just slide your feet across the ground rather than picking your feet up and putting them down, you would just bump the snake as you slid your feet and he would just move out of the way."

Joe remembered when a man by the name of Bill Dance had a TV show once a week featuring his bass fishing. So Joe asked Uncle Bert if he could compete with Bill Dance on bass fishing and he said "Yes, if they let me fish the same lakes that Dance fishes I can."

Chapter 14

Junior High and High School

FINALLY IN THE 7TH grade at the junior high school, Joe was given the opportunity to quarterback the junior high football team, but his poorly healed ankle would not allow it. Because of the pain and swelling, he was not mobile enough.

In the Meridian School System the grades were divided among campuses and that was different from most other school districts. That is, grades 7 through 10 were at Kate Griffin Junior High and grades 11 and 12 were housed in what was high school on the north campus along with the junior college, grades 13 and 14. Joe by then had switched to French horn, and he was 3rd chair. He played French horn through the 10th year of high school then wanted to challenge for the 1st chair. The band director, Mr. Howard Lawford, approved of the idea but never followed through with making it happen. This was the same treatment Joe had become accustomed to in his young life so he felt betrayed. He quit the band, but in his final year of high school decided to try out for cheerleader. He made the cheerleader squad along with six girls and one other male, John Coulter. The cheerleading year was a fun year. Joe's left ankle continued to cause problems, but he was able to dance. John Coulter and Joe were both favorites of the girls to dance with at all the dances, and both were cheerleaders.

Joe found early on that there was nothing like a good dancer to turn the girls on. He had ratted for and become a Demolay in the 10th grade. That, plus being a natural dancer, really turned the girls Joe's way. There were always dances after the football games and Joe could really put on a show for the girls. Therefore, he didn't suffer for Friday or Saturday night dates. A typical date was with one of the more popular girls, whom Joe would take to see the main movie that was playing that weekend, followed by a soft drink at one of the two drive in restaurants in town. And it was more about who you were seen with than anything else. Everyone wanted to see who was dating who, what movie and where they went after the movie. And if you were seen with the same girl very often, they might think you were 'going steady', but not many went steady in those days. Joe dated three girls fairly regularly, Mary Lou Cravitz, Lucy Holland and Sylvia Sanders, all of whom he lost contact with after high school and never saw again.

Chapter 15

College and LSU

JOE'S BEST FRIEND IN high school was Hoyt Johnson. Hoyt's Dad was manager of Sears Roebuck, and they had come from Baton Rouge a few years earlier. Hoyt was a year ahead of Joe in school, and he and his family were dyed in the wool LSU fans. Hoyt and Joe were tight, as the saying goes, and they double dated a lot. The year before Joe graduated, Hoyt and another friend of Joe's, Jimmy Pratt, graduated and left for LSU. Jimmy was the only child of a father who was a highway and bridge builder. They had money and plenty of it. Jimmy's Dad sent him off to college in a new red Pontiac convertible. Since Hoyt was going to LSU, Joe decided to go there as well. In addition, it was because his Uncle Ben, Dad's brother, had attended LSU one year before he went into the US Army in 1942.

In August of 1952, Joe was off to Baton Rouge for his freshman year and Jimmy Pratt provided the transportation in his still new Pontiac convertible. Jimmy had pledged the Kappa Sigma fraternity in his first year and was certainly instrumental in Joe getting a bid to Kappa Sigma although he did receive other bids. That's the way those kinds of things have always worked. It's always a help to have someone on the inside working for you. That's the way fraternities have always worked and always will. Joe did pledge Kappa Sigma but was sorely disappointed to find that his friend Hoyt, who had joined KS the year before, had decided to join the army for whatever reason before Joe even got there. Hoyt said he wanted to get his Army obligation behind him since they were still drafting for the Army. His intent was to return to college after his service.

While on this subject, Joe Ruff would want to say that the GI bill is one of the best programs ever coined by the Federal government because it made college graduates out of many who would otherwise never have been able to return to higher education, including himself. This was right in the middle of the Korean War, and you either went to college and made passing grades or you were drafted. Joe was not sure which was the case with Hoyt, but he knew it was either stay in college or you were drafted.

Joe would never forget when his mother and Dad came to Baton Rouge for the homecoming game between Mississippi State and LSU. Mississippi State crushed LSU 21 to 0. Joe's Dad didn't kid him too much, but he was delighted with the whipping Mississippi State gave LSU. There is an old saying among football rivals, "Just wait 'til next year!"

Academically, the first year of college was a repeat of high school. Joe thought that was a good idea at the time but when you got to the second year the party was over. It was new stuff, as Joe was soon to find out. Joe lived in the boys' dorm and there was no such thing as cohabitation with females in those days. However, his sexual curiosity was aroused by this time.

He remembered that he had a naked picture of Marilyn Monroe which he taped to the dorm wall above his bed. Now that probably would not have raised a brow nowadays. But it did back then. The Dean of men did not think it was so cool when he inspected Joe's room and saw that naked picture on the wall. He left Joe a note to take down that picture or else. And to Joe's 18 year old self he said, "It's none of your business!" And he left it right there. The next week when the Dean came through for inspection he took that picture! Joe supposed it was to hang on the Dean's own wall!!!

That year Joe took ROTC and discovered that he liked it. He learned all about drill and how to march plus officers' class room training. And he loved the uniform.

They had truly, at that time, great parties at the Kappa Sigma house, and they had a wonderful housemother, as she was called, who had her own small suite in one end of the house. Meals were served at the House and they had what he thought was the best food in town.

At the same time, Joe attended the local Christian Science Church where he met a really pretty brunette girl. She was thirty-five, but would really pass for twenty-seven if you didn't know better. She invited him over to her apartment which was located in what they called "tiger town." She lived alone and on visiting her apartment, among other chat, she shared with him that she had a seventeen year old son who was away in the Army. She and Joe got fairly close sitting on her couch and the closer they sat, the better she seemed to like it, but there was a problem; Joe didn't know what an eighteen year old boy like him was supposed to do to her or with her. Yes, Joe had sex all over his mind but didn't know what to do or exactly how to proceed. This was part of the course he had not yet had. He continued to see her, but sort of kept his distance because even as naive as he was, he felt there was a sense of danger there that he could not get past.

In the meantime, at one of the Kappa Sigma dances, and they, the fraternity, had one almost every weekend, he met Charlene Montenegro. She was also a freshman and her home was just 45 miles south of Baton Rouge, halfway to New Orleans. Her Dad owned a bar in that small town. They dated all through the spring of 1953. They would frequently ride the Ferry across from Baton Rouge to the other side of the Mississippi, the "big muddy" as it was fondly called. They would stand on the deck of the ferry and watch the lights on both sides of the river. It was indeed a romantic voyage across the river and back. He remembered one night he and Charlene were leaning against the rail kissing when suddenly they both noted that his hand was on her breast. Joe didn't know who was more surprised, him or her. In those days that was going pretty far. But at a time like that with young hormones running amuck, something like that could just happen.

Girls at that age are a lot more mature than boys, or at least in those days they were. Maybe girls received more counseling from their mothers. Joe's mother or Dad never talked with him about those things. He didn't think other boys' parents did either. Anyway, Joe would soon realize that Charlene was deadly serious about their relationship, which one could imagine created a real crisis for Joe. It was as though Joe felt pressure he needed to make a commitment to Charlene that he had not a clue of how to make. He now felt trapped. He was at a total loss. It wasn't that he didn't want to love Charlene, it was as though he was in totally unfamiliar territory. He really felt unworthy of any woman's love. He didn't know what love or commitment were and furthermore, he didn't know how to be loved. In his mind she was supposed to reject him like everyone he had ever known had done at one time or another throughout his life. And then the pattern would be complete, just like it had always played out in his life up to that time. And he simply was at a total loss. Those square pegs just would not fit into those round holes. It would take Joe many decades to put those pegs in the right holes.

Joe was taking the Pre-med curriculum, which was not easy by any stretch, but somehow he managed to make the C honor roll that year, no D'S or F's. He did remember that it was going to be a close call in Inorganic Chemistry though, and Joe paid his professor a visit to assure him that he knew enough to get a C in chemistry. And for that, everyone ended the year on a happy note. Joe had been sent off to college with his Dad's check book and he still remembered his Dad saying when he got home that in so many words, he had enjoyed being Joe's Dad, but he **could not** afford him.

The one thing Joe did not want to do was to go back to LSU for the second year. He simply could not face Charlene again . He had no cards to play.

Chapter 16

University of Houston

JOE'S GREAT AUNT AND Uncle lived in Houston, Texas and the University of Houston was there. If he transferred to the University of Houston it would be a cure for the Charlene problem. He had decided that he would move to Houston, work part-time and then go to the University of Houston part-time. He had heard it was a great party school anyway, which at the time was very important.

His great aunt was his maternal grandmother's younger sister. She and Uncle Les, her husband, were in their late fifties and had never had children of their own. Anyway, they agreed that young Joe could come live with them and go to school.

The first thing Joe did after he arrived in Houston was look for a part-time job. He found just the right job, working as a salesman at Schwobilt Clothiers, which was a men's apparel store. The store sold top of the line sport coats and suits for men with also a line of shirts and ties. It sold no clothing for women or young boys, strictly an adult men's store. There was the manager of the store, whose name was Bill, who was about fifty years of age. Bill was a nice man who always dressed well, as one would expect of the manager of a clothing store. Also, there was another man who was about thirty years of age who, like Joe, worked part time.

The owner of the store was Mr. Schwab, who was a short Jewish gentleman from Atlanta. The clothing line was made in Japan and was of the best of materials and workmanship. Most sport coats were about thirty dollars and the suits ran in price forty to fifty dollars. Mr. Schwab did visit the store while

Joe was there, and he was a nice gentleman and completely knowledgeable about the men's clothing business.

Joe scheduled fourteen semester hours of work at school and was enjoying the change of scenery. However, what would become a tragedy, evolved with Uncle Les. He was having problems with his rectum which caused him to have blood with his bowel movements. He went to see his family doctor who then referred him to a rectal surgeon who diagnosed him as having rectal cancer. This occurred during Joe's first month of living with them. Very soon it became too stressful for Uncle Les to have Joe living in the house with them, so Joe looked for another place that would be handy to the University, as well as to downtown Houston. He finally found a room with an elderly woman who had a grandson that lived with her. The grandson's name was Jerry, and he was unfriendly at first, but as time went on, they became trusting of each other, although not what Joe would call social friends. He was a little of what Joe would call 'rough around the edges', and he didn't go to college.

Meanwhile, Joe started his classes at the U of H and also took ROTC and tried out for and made the precision drill team. The drill team had special uniforms and rifles and silver helmets. They performed at football games doing special drill maneuvers. All of that was very appealing to Joe. Joe did have a very humiliating and humbling experience with the drill team at a football game though. They all knew the drill backwards and forwards so there never was any question about the members knowing exactly what they were doing. However, on this one particular evening during their half-time drill, they were doing the drill routine when the leader gave the wrong command. Joe knew better than to follow that wrong command, but under the pressure of the moment he did what the leader commanded instead of what he was supposed to do. Joe made a wrong turn which of course was obvious to the crowd. The leader later apologized for the bad command but no matter; it could not undo the bad turn which was in front of a packed stadium. Oh well, you win some and occasionally lose some, thought Joe. What an embarrassment it was to Joe though, but his friends consoled him. "These things just happen", they told him, but to Joe it seemed the end of the world again. It was so personal. His life seemed to be plagued by one disaster after another.

In the meantime, Joe was to meet his working partner at Schwobilt Clothiers, Pat Peters. Pat and Joe had an almost instant liking for each other.

Pat was married and the couple had two small children ages three and five. Joe was invited over to have dinner with them on Sunday to meet his family. His wife was a nice, attractive, early thirties lady, and Pat was thirty-three. They had been married about seven years.

During their work hours, Pat had confided in Joe that he had been a very top notch dance band drummer but had to stop playing three years earlier because he had a drinking problem. He confided that his problem was so bad that he would literally fall off the drum stool in a drunken stupor. It had now been about three years since he had played the drums. One evening after work he suggested they stop by a bar for a beer. They did, and there didn't seem to be a problem with his having a beer or two and then going home.

Finally one night Pat suggested that they stop by a nightclub where he used to play and have a beer on the way home. They did and, of course, Pat wanted Joe to see him work his magic on the drums. And play the drums he did. He was every bit as good as Gene Krupa was in his day. Problem was though, he didn't realize when he had had enough to drink. They kept drinking and the more he played after a certain point the worse he played. This drinking bout culminated in his falling of the drum stool onto the floor. That was enough. The regular drummer took back the drum playing and Pat and Joe headed out the door for home. Joe was driving and Pat kept apologizing for the embarrassing performance, not the drum performance because without the alcohol he was truly a great drummer. Joe drove him home to his wife who was not angry at him or Joe but was crying and so disappointed. She was literally crushed. And Joe felt terrible.

Joe took it a day at a time. Every day was like a new life starting all over again. But Joe was not going to like what was coming up a few days hence. It was time for the mid-semester grades to go home to Mom and Dad. There was a little problem. He was failing eleven of the fourteen hours he was taking, and how could there be a worse problem??? He was at a complete loss. The problem was that after the freshman year, the baby sitting is over and you must get your feet wet and start doing the home work and going to class. My what a mess Joe found himself in. Before he even realized it mid-term was there and what were Mom and Dad going to say?

Well sometimes things just seem to find a way to work out even though at the time it seems hopeless. Joe really did want to do the work. There just didn't seem to be enough time. But in reality, Joe had his priorities crossed . His choice of what to do now didn't seem to jive with reality.

Chapter 17

Air Force Aviation Cadet Program

ANYWAY, AS IT TURNED out, an odd thing happened at the clothing store where he was working. An Air Force Major came into the store to buy a new suit. He was dressed in Class A blues so there was no doubt he was USAF active duty. While Joe was selling him a new suit and sports coat the conversation turned to the military. Joe found out that the USAF was still training a lot of pilots through the Aviation Cadet Program and that they had dropped the educational requirement to a high school diploma. It was now November of 1953 and the US and North Korea had just agreed on a truce in June 1953 and it was shaky at best. All Joe could think about was getting his hands on the controls of one of those fighters. You may think Joe was crazy, but he still remembered those news reels when he was ten or eleven years old of those American fighter planes; and the flashes of his finger being on the trigger of those 50 caliber machine guns just sent cold chills through his body. He felt like this was deliverance for him. And danger? He never gave it a single thought.

Joe asked the Major, "How do I sign up?" And the Major said, "Easy. Just see the Air Force recruiter, and they will transport you over to Lackland Air Force Base at San Antonio, Texas." And that was only about 200 miles away. "There they will test you and do a physical exam, and if you pass, you will be given a class assignment and a reporting date." It just so happened that the Major was a pilot flying T29s at Ellington ABF in Houston for the purpose of training Navigators.

Over the next week, Joe was able to get all the testing done and headed home to Meridian, Mississippi, the following week. WOW, what a relief it would be to tell his parents that all was not lost, and he would be heading to the USAF to train to be an Air Force jet pilot and a gentleman.

When Joe got home, his parents were now aware of his grades and he received a less than warm welcome; but they were at least resolute to the situation their son had created for himself. By then they realized that Joe must be allowed to be Joe. But whether Joe knew who Joe was, was a whole 'nother question, as we shall see later.

By the time Joe got home it was just about Thanksgiving. The retail stores were hiring Christmas help and he was hired by the leading clothing retailer in town for the Christmas rush. Joe was working downstairs selling shirts, ties and other men's wear. He was now nineteen. He met a lady working in the same department named June. She was very friendly and knew his family. They became good friends and had lunch together quite often. In fact, Joe found her quite attractive. She had brown hair and brown eyes and her teeth were attractive as was her mouth and lips. Different strokes for different folks, but Joe knew he wanted a sexy looking woman. He was a legs and ass guy, but she needed to have a pretty face and mouth as well. He was pretty choosey about who he would be seen with. June was five feet five inches tall and weighed 110 pounds. One day they were just kidding when no customers were around and she looked at Joe and said "I'll met you half way." Well for sure he'd been around enough by now to know what that meant. She was thirty-five, she was not married, and she lived alone. This turned out to be Joe's first encounter with real sex and educate him she did. Among other things she taught him that sex was a two-sided coin. Most people probably know that young boys start masturbating at age thirteen to fifteen. What masturbating teaches a boy is that sex is all about self gratification, since there is no female partner involved. Usually masturbating comes a little later for girls, but it's not just a male thing. It works for both sexes. Later in life Joe would meet a woman who could masturbate by bouncing her foot off the floor carpet of the car floor. So Joe had no idea of how to approach this sexual relationship. At first it's WHAM BAM THANK YOU MA'M, and I'm out of here. Joe, like most his peers, approached sex in this way. It didn't take long though for her to teach him that the sexual act was for both parties, and that the object of the act was for both parties to mutually have a great and complete orgasm. He soon learned how the timing of the moment brought maximum advantage for both of them. And once he mastered that part, they had a wonderful sexual relationship.

It was no secret that 19-year-old Joe was getting educated so both of them could make the most of the time they had together. She, for certain, knew that Joe was soon to be off to officer and pilot training with the USAF and certainly both of them knew that their love affair was over with the day he departed for the USAF on January 21, 1954. But they both were in denial that the day was soon to arrive; after which, chances were that they would never cross paths again. This little fling would last until Joe left for the Air Force in late January of 1954. Joe had had his first sexual odyssey with a real grown up woman sixteen years his senior. But the main thing was that he thought for the first time he had found a female that understood him and his inner workings. She never was critical or demeaning to him. She was a real cougar in the finest sense of the word. Joe had for sure lost his virginity and now was beginning to understand at least part of the underpinnings of love, not all of it, but at least how the sexual part is but a small part of the big picture. He certainly realized by now that great sex was part of, but not the only part, of love making and how sex and other acts of love go together to make a whole lasting relationship. This is not to belittle sexless relationships, but simply to say that sex plays a more or lesser role in the lives of lovers, depending on where they are in their lives at the moment.

Time was getting short. Joe's departure was only about two weeks away. Joe and his mother were in Weidman's restaurant late one evening having a piece of their renowned black bottom pie when Joe looked at his mother and said that he had decided not to go to the Air Force but would rather go to the Juilliard School of Music and study music. And yes, you could have heard a pin drop. His mother looked him straight in the eye and said in a firm voice, "YOU ARE GOING TO THE AIR FORCE!!!" Joe said, "But what if I get killed in a plane crash??" "YOU ARE GOING TO THE AIR FORCE!!" was his mother's reply. And that was the last time that was discussed. In other words it was time for Joe to start and finish something. And Joe's hindsight later would cause him to agree with this.

Chapter 18

Triangular Relationship

THERE WAS SOME BACKGROUND to this situation with Joe's mother. When Joe was born, he was, as we've said before, the second of two boys; and since Brick was the bigger, stronger, and more outgoing of the two, Joe's mother somehow felt the need to come to the rescue of the underdog, scrawny little Joe. Where this led throughout his life with his mother though was that she was his protector more than a mother. And this eventually grew into a greater problem. Mother and Joe became best friends instead of mother and son. She would tell Joe about her personal problems with Dad and recruit him as her ally. Of course, Dad picked up on this at an early point, and he became extremely paranoid and jealous of Joe. In his jealousy and paranoia, Dad learned to hate Joe. It was not just Joe that he hated, it was anyone that Joe's mother showed any affection for, male or female, even her lady friends. So what Joe did was try to stay out of his Dad's way and by all means stay away from him as much as possible. At times Joe's Dad would try to make amends in his own way by talking with Joe and asking him to ride up to one of the farms with him. And Joe tried to do his part by accepting the offer, but it was guaranteed that Joe would have a migraine by the time he got home from the ride. With Dad it was just a non starter. All three of them, Mom, Joe and Dad were stuck in an unhealthy triangular relationship. As it turned out, at least for the moment, Joe's departure for the Air Force was none the less a God send.

This negative relationship with Joe's Dad was not a new thing. When Joe was a senior in high school, for one reason or another, Joe's Dad had stayed out most of the night drinking at a nite club called Skyview Inn which sat on the very top of a hill just south of Meridian. Joe didn't know what was going on between Dad and Mom at the moment but unfortunately while driving down the side of that curvy road from the Inn, it was raining. and Dad's car went into a skid. Unfortunately, the driver's door flew open, and he fell out of the car onto the wet pavement, and in the process the driver's side rear wheel rolled over his pelvis. That was his only injury though, a fractured pelvis.

Of course, you know there were no seat belts in cars in those days. The news, and I mean the whole news, spread all over their little town and the whole family, knowing the details, was extremely embarrassed. And young people like Joe were extremely sensitive and embarrassed that his Dad had done such a thing.

Joe and his mother visited his Dad the next day and found that he was in a lot of pain but not the least bit repentant. The whole thing struck a bad note with Joe. Joe didn't know how to respond except by facial expression, and his Dad picked up on that immediately. When his Dad got home, he had to use a large cattle prod for a walking stick to get around the house. You know, the kind one uses to prod cattle with. One night the three of them, Mom, Dad and Joe, were seated at the dinner table for the evening meal. Joe said something about the accident and how embarrassed he was about it at school. Suddenly his Dad rose from his seat and was going to hit Joe with the stick when Joe's mother jumped between them. Joe was stunned, but not surprised, at his Dad's response; stunned that he would actually strike such a blow at him. That stick was a lethal weapon. And this would be the last time, as a young boy, that Joe would ever speak to his Dad without carefully choosing his words. From then on their relationship would be distantly estranged, to say the least.

Chapter 19

USAF Class 55M

JOE LEFT HOME FOR THE Air Force on January 22, 1954, arriving at Lackland Air Force Base, San Antonio, Texas on January 24, 1954, two days ahead of his mandatory reporting date. Joe was soon to learn what life was like for a new lower classman in preflight school.

Since Joe was the first one of the new class, class 55M, to arrive, he learned really soon that there was a party going on. But it wasn't his party. It was the party of the upper classmen, and he and the others soon to arrive were their new toys. He had breakfast with his upper classmen the day before the rest of his class arrived, and boy did they enjoy jumping on the only new recruit before the rest of his classmates arrived the next day. Arriving early had one advantage, as Joe saw it, and that was he got to pick which bunk he would have for the next twelve weeks. Joe would never forget the first morning he went to breakfast with his upper class. They showed him everything from table manners to how he must seat himself at the table. And just to make it more fun, Joe found a piece of chewing gum in his scrambled eggs. But the fun was just beginning for 55J Class, who would be his masters for the next six weeks, after which they would depart for the flight training bases and class 55M would become the upper class. But that would prove to be light years away.

Joe would never forget that first morning that all the newbie's of class 55M were all standing by their bunk beds, one above and one below. Joe had the bottom bunk, second bed on the left as you would walk from the latrine. They were formally given their bunk assignments, and each Cadet received a foot locker in which all of his belongings were to go. It had an upper lift out portion and a lower part where larger items were to be stored. Everything had its exact spot in which it had to be located, from toilet articles, shaving gear, underwear, shirts, pants, socks, tee shirts, etc. Some of the uniform items had to be hung on an open hanger space. Everything was Air Force issue: belts, buckles, shoes and a pair of Air Force boots. All buckles, boots and shoes had to be spit shined and you'd better be able to see yourself in the toes of those boots and shoes. There was not to be a speck of dust anywhere and they had white glove inspections. There was a system of demerits for any discrepancies that were found by the upper classmen. Joe remembered well the first week that he was there when everyone got to go to the Cadet Club, have a few beers and see the girls. Little did Joe know that the first time at the Cadet Club would be his last time in three months that he would see the inside of it while he was at Lackland AFB. You see, getting to go to the Cadet Club on Saturdays and Sundays was directly linked to how many demerits one had accrued during the week prior. It was also possible that one could receive so many demerits in a few days that that Cadet might not be able to ever go to the Cadet Club. This was the case with Joe. He just could not seem to do anything right. And there was one upper classman in particular who seemed to enjoy staying on Joe's case. So those who had demerits had to march up and down in front of headquarters an hour for each demerit they had accrued over a specific number. One might think that if you had a weak spot, the upper classmen would pounce on it until it bled. One upper classman would get right in his face and scream ugly remarks trying to make him break. But you must stay stony faced and only answer, "Yes sir!" or "No sir!", unless a specific question was asked. And if you had an answer, it better be the one he was looking for.

Latrine duty was assigned on a daily basis, and if it was your day for latrine duty, that was an extra added liability for you that day since they were good at finding something wrong with the cleanliness of the bathroom. The men stood at inspection by their bunks and that blanket on your bed had better be on there tight enough to bounce a quarter coin in the air.

Joe would have to admit that his past history of betrayal by almost everyone he knew made this a very difficult time. He should have looked at the whole thing as a big joke and laughed it off for the fun and jokes that it really was, but no , he took it all personal as though he really was the no good SOB that the upper classman at the moment was making him out to be. The guys like Wendell Downs from Los Angeles, who was a little older at the time , twenty-two to be exact, did well because he, along with most of the rest, took the hazing in a good natured, joking kind of way. Some of them would actually break down laughing while being hazed. But not Mom's boy. Joe took it as personal . How unfortunate at the time . But times and things have a way of turning around as the players change.

Along with marching drills, and physical training in the mornings, inspections and academics in the afternoons, it was a busy schedule, and Joe never had time off just to do nothing in particular. But after six weeks then Joe's class became the upper class. He didn't have anyone that he especially wanted to harass so he was more helpful to the new cadets than threatening. He just wanted to move on.

Later years would have Joe look back on this hazing in preflight with a positive feeling. Maybe it was a bit mentally brutal for a reason. Maybe it was to test you under pressure to see if you would crack under the stress of combat. But he certainly didn't want to ever repeat that experience. And later he thought the student officers, as they were dubbed, were really short-changed by not having to go through preflight training as the cadets did.

There were two possibilities for assignments from preflight training. You either went to pilot training or navigator training. And this was determined when you were first tested before you went into the Air Force. All the pilot trainees went to one of three or four possible bases to receive exactly the same training. If you were a pilot trainee, it was only a matter of in what part of the country you preferred to have your training.

Joe had heard a lot about Arizona and its dry climate, so he picked Marana Air Base at Marana, Arizona as his choice. He was excited to get his choice. But first he needed to return home to Mississippi to pick up a car to drive. His Dad had arranged for him to buy a car that Dad's brother had owned. Joe was glad to get it. It was a 1950 Studebaker coup, which his Uncle Ralph had outgrown, so to speak.

Chapter 20

Primary Flight Training

SO JOE ARRIVED AT HIS new flight base on about May 1, 1954. As he drove in the gate, the first thing he saw was a sign that said Darr Aero Tech Primary flight school. This would be Joe's home base for the next six months. The flight school was a civilian flight contractor who was contracted by the Air Force to do what was called PRIMARY flight training of Air Force pilots.

It just so happened that the 55M class was the first Air Force or Navy pilots to be trained in tricycle landing gear only. All other prior classes had been trained in what was called 'tail draggers' first, followed later by tricycle gear training. This only made sense because all air planes being built were tricycle anyway, so why waste time flying 'tail draggers' when you will never fly them again. None the less, this class 55M made history.

All cadets were housed in small buildings where there was room for six men with nicer and more private rooms. The buildings surrounded the parade grounds and gone forever were the days of being hazed by some jerk that got there six weeks before you did. The cadets were there to learn, and there were several classes on the base at the same time, but everyone was equal. On the east end of the parade grounds was the Cadet Club where everyone hung after hours unless you thought you had studying that you needed to do. Inside it was a typical nightclub, booths, tables and a bar, and it was only open on the weekends, beginning at 4 pm Friday.

Everyone was there to learn to fly those airplanes parked on that flight line. The flight line was on the west end of the parade area and the mess hall was also on the west end of the complex, but the cafeteria was slightly east of the flight line. There were one or two classrooms located among the barracks buildings where the academic classes were held. The ground school instructors were real professionals and really knew their subject matter.

Everyone started right away on learning the flight systems and the theory of flight, that is, what exactly causes the wing of an aircraft to develop lift; and that it's not the pressure under the wing but the vacuum that builds up above the wing that causes the wing to develop lift. They learned much more about the T34 aircraft engine, fuel system, controls and variable pitch propellers. They also had to know that aircraft inside and out, everything about it . That's what pilots do, and that is why it is a profession all its own.

Meanwhile, the cadets were divided into two flights at the flight line, the Demons and the Polecats. Each flight had their separate building and there were about ten tables and ten instructors in each building, and there were three or four students at each table with an instructor pilot.

Joe's instructor was strictly a good old boy born and raised in Tucson, which was only 30 miles south of Marana. His name was Andy Anderson . He had been an enlisted man pilot during WW2 and Tucson was his home. He was a Mormon from the grass roots. He did not drink, smoke or ever say a nasty word or even raise his voice. He literally conducted himself as a saint. A nicer man Joe had never met. He was born and raised in North Tucson in an area called Binghamton. It was an all Mormon community and he and his wife had five children from about age ten down to diapers. Joe was to visit his clan on one occasion and found that his wife was a pleasantly plump, very plain, but also very sweet, person. And the children were all very well mannered.

One might wonder how such a large group of Mormons happened to settle in Tucson. It happened because the reason the Mormons moved west to begin with is that they were practicing in plural marriage and they chose the Salt Lake Valley because when Brigham Young looked out over the valley for the first time he said from his wagon, "This is the place." But then how did they get to Tucson? The practice of plural marriage brought the wrath of the Federal government down upon them and so Brigham Young countered by spreading them out towards Tucson, St. George and Idaho, so they could survive the onslaught of the Federal troops.

Meanwhile back at the flight line, Andy had three students, including Joe. They would be the first class to fly the T34, which was built by Beechcraft, a company which would later become Raytheon, and a company that would later also become an almost exclusively military weapons producer.

UP UNTIL NOW THEY HAD only built commercial aircraft, but they were known to be of the highest quality aircraft ever built. The T34 was nothing more than a V-tailed Bonanza with a conventional tail and tandem seating, student in the front seat and instructor in the rear seat. In other words, instead of having two parts or surfaces for the tail, it had three, two horizontal surfaces and also a vertical tail or rudder which made it easier to fly and control for student pilots.

By the way, the Beechcraft was commonly flown by civilians. And do you know why they call the Beechcraft aircraft the doctor killer? It's because any doctor that ever had fantasies about flying buys himself a Beechcraft Bonanza once he has the money to do so. And he thinks that all he has to do is read a few books about flying, and he suddenly becomes a genius of flight. Some lawyers fit that category as well. Then the next thing he does is fly the damn thing into bad weather, and the aircraft comes apart, and what's left of him hits the ground with "great exuberance", and that's the end of the story of why the Bonanza came by the nick name of "the doctor killer."

The early flights in the aircraft were controlled more by the instructor from the back seat with the student gradually taking the controls as soon as he was capable. Joe and his instructor would go to the designated practice area and practice making level turns in both directions. The instructor would demonstrate how the torque of the engine affected the aircraft in turns and how to compensate for torque at low speeds and at faster speeds. He taught you how to use the throttle and rudder in all situations effectively. They would then practice stalls and proper stall recovery. Later, they would practice touch and go landings with the instructor giving the student as much control of the aircraft as the student could handle at the time. Of course, this was all leading up to the point that the instructor would have the student taxi the aircraft back to the ramp, where the instructor would unstrap himself, get out of the air craft and say, "Now, you go solo and show me how to take off and land this aircraft."

Well, many of the student pilots soloed by eight or ten hours dual time. But not Joe, he was like a lost ball in high weeds. He wasn't near ready to solo by ten or even twelve hours. His instructor thought Joe could do this but not Joe. By the time Joe had twelve hours, he was at the breaking point. He either had to solo in the next two or three hours or he would have to be washed out of the program. Joe's instructor knew he could do it. If he could just get Joe to believe in himself he could take charge and do it.

Finally after fifteen hours of dual instruction, Andy took the bull by the horns, got out of the airplane and said, "Go do it. Go do two touch and goes and do a full stop land on the third one." Joe took off and made a closed pattern and came down final approach much too fast and touched down way too fast, bounced three or four feet in the air and pushed the power full on, then retracted the gear and went for another closed pattern. The results were a little better on the 2nd attempt, but he was still too fast on down final approach, resulting in still another bouncy, terrible landing. Joe gave it full power again and did another closed pattern for a full stop landing this time. He was still too fast and it was a rough landing, but Joe did get back on the ground all in one piece. Joe was probably the last one in his class to solo. But he had never been a quitter, and there had to be better days ahead.

Everyone was doing these practice landings at one of the Aux fields. Joe stopped the aircraft. Andy got back in the back seat and simply said, "Lets go home." That would be the last scary time Joe would ever have in an aircraft. After that he knew he could do it, and Andy knew he could do it too. Joe flew it back to home base and flew that airplane like he owned it. That would be the last time there would ever be any challenge to Joe's competence to fly any aircraft. Flying airplanes is a lot like riding a bicycle, if you can ride one of them you can ride any of them. He now had the self-confidence that there was no airplane he couldn't master; not only that, he surpassed all his classmates in flying after that. He now had the confidence in his own ability that early life experiences had robbed him of. He felt like he was finally **king of the hill!**

Everyone was scheduled to fly the T34 for forty hours total and continued to work on their proficiency at all basic flight maneuvers that are considered fundamental to flying. So this would take a couple of months along with continued class room instruction of the theory of flight, fundamental aircraft design and this would be their opening start in that phenomenon called weather training. If there is one place that pilots who are not military trained really fall short, it is the intensive training that military pilots receive on weather training. This gets more pilots killed in civil aviation than any other single thing. They simply can't find the same training that military pilots routinely receive. It would take these pilots about two months to finish the T34 program.

Following this, these pilots would fly the T28, which was also sitting right there on the ramp waiting for them when they arrived. The T28 was a much larger aircraft than the T34. It was very imposing as far as size was concerned. Where the T34 was an aircraft that weighed about 2500 lbs with no fuel, the T28 weighed about 6000 lbs with no fuel, so its size was somewhat imposing compared to the T34. But Joe thought if you can fly one of them, you can fly any of them. The T28 was built by North American and was a two seater like the T34. It had an 800 horsepower engine though to lug all that weight around. The Navy had a version of the same airplane that had a 1200 horse engine and by comparison, the Air Force version was woefully under powered. It saw limited action in the Korean War and had been mostly retired from service because the Air Force and the Navy had both gone to jets by now.

JOE'S TRANSITION TO the T28 was smooth and just like falling off an old log. He soloed right away and was flying and doing what he thought he was born to do. One of the things they did in the T28 that they did not do in the T34 was fly what was called round robin cross countries. That's where you plan a route using a map, and you fly to one point, usually a town, then you take up a new heading and fly to another point, and after you have made several check points, you then turn to a heading that takes you back to home base. Picacho Peak is an odd shaped small peak that is easily recognized from 30 or so miles away, and the instructors all told us that if we felt disoriented or lost, to always look around for Picacho Peak.

Anyway, on Joe's 1st round robin cross country a little redheaded short guy by the name of Petenpaul got lost and one of the roving in-flight instructors had to go pick him up and guide him home. This was not an uncommon occurrence. It happened quite often. Every one of the guys kidded him about getting lost but especially Joe.

A week or so later they had another cross country and guess who got lost. Yes, you got it right, it was Joe. Boy did Joe catch hell for that. The instructor pilot that went out and picked Joe up found him at Ajo, Arizona, a small copper mining town in southwest Arizona. And what do you think the caption under Joe's picture in the Annual book said? "Lost at Ajo? No, I got kinfolks there." Joe wanted to be fair to himself though. What actually happened was that his electronic gyro was thirty degrees out of phase, and that's why he was flying 30 degrees off the correct heading, and that's why he flew way off course. He knew early on that there was a problem, but he didn't know to double check the electronic heading indicator with the B16 magnetic compass. And up to that point he had never thought about that small detail. The B16 magnetic compass is NEVER wrong unless you are at extreme high latitudes near the north or south poles. You better believe he learned a most meaningful lesson, one that could well save his life. This was a lesson he would never forget. He didn't remember this ever being talked about in class but he should have read it in the flight manual. This would never happen to Joe again. He was never lost in an aircraft again over the many years that he flew them.

This group also began instrument training in the T28. The aircraft was equipped with a white hood in the rear seat that could be pulled forward to shut out the outside of the aircraft so that whoever was in the back seat could only see the instruments. This was called 'flying under the hood.' Andy and Joe had done several instrument rides before. One day Andy told him to make a 180 degree turn to the right at 3 degrees per second , hold the same airspeed and climb at 500 feet per minute. This would mean that he would need to add a small amount of throttle to hold the air speed constant while turning at 3 degrees per second. In doing this maneuver, Joe would climb 500 ft and turn exactly 180 degrees in the direction he was turning. In other words he would climb 500 feet while completely reversing the direction of flight. Joe did several of those exercises, following which Andy told Joe to come out from under the hood, and they headed back toward the home base. Andy was quiet for a moment and then he said, "Joe, you are the best student I have ever taught instrument flying to." Joe was so excited he almost jumped out of the airplane at 8000 ft. But Joe did; he naturally took to flying on instruments. It was easy, always believe the instruments, and make small corrections and TRIM, TRIM,TRIM. In other words keep all the pressure off the stick by trimming the elevator in particular. If you are a good instrument pilot you fly the aircraft WITH YOUR FINGER TIPS ONLY ON THE CONTROL STICK. Don't ever jerk or snatch the aircraft around. If you do that you better only fly on nice days when you have good visibility. Surprisingly, a lot of those types did manage to get through the program. Joe knew that he was a natural at instrument flying from early on. He likened instrument flying to dealing with a pretty woman. You read her right and make small corrections. Class 55M would remain at Marana Air Base, just north of Tucson until about the end of October 1954. And by the end of the Marana Air Base tour, Joe and his class mates had logged approximately 100 hours of student pilot time.

Joe's social life while at Marana was just as rich as his flying experience. The very first Sunday Joe was at Marana he made his appearance at the Tucson Christian Science Church. He was there specifically to make social contacts, which he did. He met a friend for life, Mike Lawford, who at the time was in his junior year at Tucson High. Mike lived with his mother and younger brother, Herb, who was thirteen at the time. Mike was seventeen. He was very outgoing but was not an athlete in any sense. He was on the fencing team and was quite good at it . He was the top fencer at Tucson High. He was also a straight A student. Of course Mike invited Joe over to meet his mother and brother and Joe felt immediately at home. He also had a sister who was twenty, but she was living and traveling in Europe at the time. They lived on Speedway Blvd. near the University of Arizona. His mother's name was Betty and the three of them lived alone. Mile's father had brought them to Arizona eight years earlier from North Carolina. Story was that the father had brought them to Tucson and returned to North Carolina to finish up some business odds and ends and for whatever reason, he supported them but never returned to Tucson.

Mike and Joe became great friends and saw each other every weekend. There were also several girls in the church that Mike knew well and they would entertain them on weekends. Mike's home was a second home to Joe, and Joe had a car and that made them mobile. They frequently had pizza and beer on Saturday and would take the girls on picnics to places like Sabino Canyon, which was about 10 miles out of town at the foot of Mt. Lemon.

Also, they frequently drove to the top of Mt. Lemon where there was a beautiful old lodge they loved to visit. The road up the mountain was paved only half way in those days, the last half was gravel. The old lodge was rustic and decorated in typical old western style, including a huge open fire place with what appeared to be old pine floors and old but uniquely nice western style furniture. Joe remembered that it was always cool up there, even in the hot summer. And when fall arrived there was nothing as satisfying as standing in front of that warm fire place. Joe was in love with old Tucson, commonly known as the "old Pueblo."

At the time, Tucson was a city of about 90,000, and it was so exclusive that one might think that there was no life outside itself. It was just a grand place to be, not too large or too small. But the "old Pueblo' did its own thing, not too much government and not too little. And it was only 60 miles from the Mexican border, so if you wanted to do so, you could go to Nogales and visit across the border or have a new pair of western boots custom made. Tucson was 2680 feet above sea level, so the summers were not nearly as hot as Phoenix, which was only 120 miles north. Also the humidity was much lower in Tucson making the days even cooler.

In those days there were no interstates though there were some four lane roads. By 1960 however all this would change with the new interstate infrastructure built mainly during the administration of President Eisenhower.

Chapter 21

Basic Pilot Training - Williams AFB

THE NEXT STOP ON JOE'S odyssey in pilot training would be Williams AFB, located at Chandler, Arizona. Chandler was a small town of about 5000 people, and was the home of Arizona State University. This time there was a choice between Greenville AFB and Williams AFB, and Joe loved the weather and life in the west and wanted to stay there. At this point, the students were given a choice between single or multi engine training. The multi engine students would go to B25 school, and the single engine students would fly the T33 and be placed at Williams AFB at Chandler, Arizona, or Greenville AFB in Mississippi.

When Joe arrived at Williams AFB, he was impressed by the cleanliness of the grounds and buildings. The buildings were painted in a beige color, and the barracks were typical in appearance of WW2 buildings, but looked so clean and pristine. The grass was all mowed and well kept. It was a beautifully kept facility. Joe drove by the headquarters building and, of course, the Cadet Club. It was a beautiful place, and Joe's barracks was just across the street from it.

There were two cadets to a room and the beds were typical military single bunk beds. Each cadet had his own area for his hanging clothes and a table style desk. The latrine was a community type but was well kept. Joe's roommate turned out to be a young guy from New Hampshire. Joe couldn't help but note that he brought his snow skis with him though Joe didn't know where this guy thought he would use them in the middle of the desert, not to mention the time to use them. Anyway, what does a redneck from Mississippi know? Well, his name was Guy Barker, and he was a real talker and authority on everything. But they hit it off right away and got along well. And Joe could hardly wait to get his hands on the controls of the T33, his first jet to fly.

By now the cadets were well aware of what they were there for. They were there to learn to fly combat aircraft and the baby sitting was over. From here on out it was all business. You would not be flying with a civilian instructor; all the instructors were military pilots, many of whom were returnees from the Korean War. So many of them had already looked the enemy straight in the eye.

The academics were the same as before, but the aircraft systems were more complicated, and the new guys had to know them by heart. The weather classes were the same as before, but with many more particulars that were intensely taught.

The flight line was the same but with the difference being the type of aircraft and more special procedures. Joe and his fellow cadets would start with the T28, which they would fly for another 40 hours, after which they would transition into jets, the T33.

The instructors were all Air Force pilots and all other personnel were regular Air Force too. The cadets did fall into formation to march back and forth to class and the flight line, and, as when they were at the primary base, each instructor did have a separate table and two or three students. Joe's instructor was 1st Lieutenant Pennell and there was one other student at his table named John Ames. John and Joe would become close friends and remain so for years to come.

Before they could fly the aircraft, they had to get the ground school done for that particular aircraft. Since they had already flown the T28, the ground school for it was short. The first flight was, as always, an orientation flight, which was primarily an orientation of the locale. One of the things Joe's instructor pointed out was the close proximity of the surrounding populated areas and also any mountain structures that might be a factor in night flying, in particular Camelback Mountain. Camelback was just on the north edge of Scottsdale. The location of Scottsdale to Camelback Mountain would come up again later.

The T28 phase went by at a snail's pace for Joe. By now he knew this aircraft inside and out and was proficient at all phases of flying it. One of the things the student pilots had to do was shoot a series of eight or ten touch and go landings in front of the mobile control unit, which was placed just to the side of the active runway. Joe shot eight touch and go landings perfectly placed right in front of the mobile control unit, which was located exactly 1000 feet down the runway. He literally put on a 'landing the aircraft clinic', enough so that Captain Sarver, commander of the flight, had him stand during preflight briefing the next morning and awarded him ten gold stars on the chart that stood in front of the room where all the student pilots' names were listed.

Captain Sarver was an older pilot with Korean experience and was highly thought of. Usually instructor pilots got their pick of assignments after doing a tour in Korea and doing a tour as a flight instructor. Captain Sarver would later go to F84F training at Luke AFB just outside Phoenix.

Once class 55M started in the T33, Joe felt like he had finally made it to heaven.

THE T33 WAS THE TWO seat version of the F80 Shooting Star, which was used some during the Korean War mainly for air to ground warfare. In the T34 and the T28 the cadets did spins in order to practice recovery from unintentional spins which could happen if the airspeed got too low and the controls were mishandled. However spins were not practiced in the T33.

There was only one instructor in their flight who would spin the T33. Of course his name was Rocky, and his call sign when in flight formation was Rock flight. Joe thought Rock was one cool guy. He was six feet tall and had a pencil mustache and not an once of fat. Joe asked Rock if he would make a flight with him and spin the T33. Rock said, "Sure." They did make that flight, and it was fun though the T- bird, as it was called, sort of wallowed and flattened out at one point, and this flat spinning characteristic was the reason why most pilots would not spin it. It took a lot of altitude to recover, so you wouldn't want to spin it at low altitude because when spinning, the recovery was much slower. Maybe that's why Rock climbed to 30,000 feet to start the spin. It was fun, but Joe learned that you would never want to get the T-bird into a spin at low altitude, unless of course you planned to eject, but never mind, if you got out alive you would then be the subject of a flying evaluation board (FEB), and that would end your flying career unceremoniously.

As time and a little more experience would prove, Joe was becoming an especially good all round pilot and an excellent instrument pilot. That means flying in the weather where you had to rely only on the cockpit instruments to fly the aircraft. He was also an excellent formation pilot. In order to graduate from pilot training, flight check rides were required for general proficiency and an instrument flight check as well. Joe had his instrument flight check with Captain Joseph, who worked at Flight Headquarters. This was one of those days that Joe could do no wrong during his flight check and Captain Joseph gave him a T-score of 82 which Captain Joseph said was the highest grade he had ever given a student.

At this point in Joe's training, he was feeling a little bit bulletproof, which probably was not unusual for one who is not quite twenty-one. And as a result a little bit of a rub developed between Joe and his instructor. His instructor was shy to the point of Joe wondering if he wasn't just a little bit fearful of flying. Joe later reflected back on a flight when they were practicing no flap landings. Joe flew the pattern just perfectly, but his instructor kept pushing the power up and saying, "You are going to land short." In all fairness though, you cannot see as well from the back seat as you can from the front because the nose of the aircraft has to come up higher than usual. So, it puts the man in the rear seat at a disadvantage because its like he's sitting in a hole where he cannot see out front as well. Also the speed on base leg and final approach will be about 10 knots faster.

Anyway the instructor couldn't see as well and kept pushing the throttle forward, and Joe kept pulling it back to idle in sort of a tug of war. He'd say, "You are short!" And Joe says, "We are not short. I've got it!" Well, end of story, Joe landed 1200 feet down the runway in a perfect landing. Joe's instructor was not happy, but he was wrong. He just couldn't see from the back. But his instructor, Lt. Pernell, did take it personal and from that point on, he was cool towards Joe.

Every Friday night a bus load of young ladies would arrive at the Cadet Club for the weekly dance party. One of the young ladies Joe met in the early going was Janet Munch. She was a pretty blonde, had blue eyes and was about 5 feet 4 inches tall. She probably weighed about 115 pounds. What a coincidence that she was a Christian Scientist as well. Her family also attended the Christian Science church. Her father fed cattle for their living and always had several pens of cattle. That gave Joe something in common with her Dad since Joe's Dad was a cattle broker. Janet and Joe had some wonderful times together. One date in the early going stood out. They decided to eat at one of the expensive restaurants in Phoenix and only after being seated at the table did Joe remember to look in his wallet to find that he had only five dollars. They both laughed it off, and Joe embarrassingly asked the waiter what he could buy with five dollars. He said a large salad. So that's what they had. Janet was to graduate from Scottsdale High that year and was planning to attend the University of Arizona in Tucson. One night when Joe was night flying he decided to buzz Janet's home in Scottsdale. He was heading southeast from northwest at 500 feet above the ground when he suddenly noted this big black spot right in front of him. Guess what that black spot was. Camelback Mountain. He did an immediate hard G pull-up and said to himself, "I'll never do anything like that again!"

But there was a problem with the relationship with Janet and it was that same old problem Joe had before, the one called commitment. He had a real problem with commitment. Somehow he was terrified of total commitment to any woman. Maybe it was his pathological relationship with his mother that kept him estranged from serious relationships with women. With his mother it was I love you now followed by no I don't love you now because you have done something to disappoint me. So Joe just could not unconditionally trust any woman. He did not understand this about himself until many years later. It was as though in his subconscious mind he couldn't trust any woman to know the real Joe. He would ultimately be rejected. So, as long as the relationship was superficial, she could count Joe in.

But now the relationship with Janet had gotten to the put up or shut up point, and Joe began to push her away. Janet was a great girl, pretty, and she had a good head, but she needed a man to match her maturity. This, at the moment, Joe didn't have. He subconsciously pushed her away. He stopped calling.

Meanwhile he would meet another nice lady at the Cadet Club Friday night dance event, Linda Stricker. Her father was a prominent attorney in Phoenix and that was a good thing for what was about to happen. Lisa was a pretty brunette, about 5 feet 2 inches tall and weighed all of 100 pounds. Joe had never had a fetish for fat girls even though his Dad had always laughingly said, "Fat girls are better because there is more of them to love." During the dance that night Joe and Linda decided he would drive her home rather than her going on the bus that had brought the ladies to the dance party. Joe and Linda departed the Cadet Club shortly after 1 AM when the dance was over. Joe and Linda had both had several drinks during the course of the evening, but neither of them were intoxicated.

Linda lived in Phoenix, which was about 20 miles away. They drove north to Mesa and across through Tempe and continued on to Van Buren in Phoenix headed west. Van Buren was the widest street in Phoenix at that time. It was four lane and they did allow parking along the outside westbound lane. Joe had been up since 5am that morning because they had an early inspection and parade that morning. He was very sleepy. Linda was sitting close to him and he had his arm around her. He noticed he was having difficulty with nodding out and then he would awaken fully, so he slowed his car down to about 25 miles per hour. He thought he was wide awake, and then suddenly they veered to the right side of the road, and the crash of hitting a parked car from the rear woke him from his sleep.

Joe was not hurt in any way, but Linda had sustained a two inch laceration just below her knee cap. It would later need to have a few sutures. Soon the police came and when they smelled alcohol on Joe's breath, they smelled blood in the water. There were several young officers and you would have thought they had just captured John Dillinger or Pretty Boy Floyd. They said Joe was drunk as soon as they got there. They had him walk a straight line, which he did; and they had him walk putting one foot immediately in front of the other, which he was able to do. They asked him for his license and he told them he was a Cadet. They relished all this even more. They never had him blow up a balloon nor did they take a blood alcohol level, but they were determined to throw him in the drunk tank. Lisa pleaded with them, but to no avail. They wanted to lock Joe up.

And so it was. They put him in the drunk tank and didn't even tell Joe if Linda got home alright. That afternoon around 4 PM the Air Police came and picked Joe up and took him back to the base. This was only one month before Joe's scheduled graduation from pilot training.

When Linda's father was told by Linda what had occurred, he simply called and had the drunk driving charge removed. Joe was too embarrassed to even call Linda's father and thank him for what he had done. And Joe was too ashamed to even call Linda back after that.

Meanwhile, back at the flight line, the cadets were finishing up loose ends and getting ready to go to their next assignment. The Air Force had promised all who signed on for an additional year that they would get advanced training after graduation. It was not until graduation that they found out that the Air Force lies a lot too. They had too many graduates to make good on the promises. What they didn't say was what kind of advanced training. Everyone assumed that since they had been trained in single engine jets that it would be some kind of single engine jet. Not so, there were about six fighter jet slots for about fifty pilots. So most of the class was sent to some sort of multiengine program which the Air Force called or labeled "advanced training."

Chapter 22

Advanced Training B26

JOE WAS SENT TO THE B-26 program at Enid Oklahoma for an eight week transition program. This was the so-called advanced training that he signed an extra year for. How disgusting! The B26 had been used extensively in Korea for air to ground support. During his eight week stay at Enid AFB, he would find some of the aircraft had bullet holes in them that had never been repaired. Joe tried to make the best of the situation. The B26 was a good aircraft though, reciprocating engine or not. It cruised at 200 mph on one engine or the same speed with two engines running. It was a vastly overpowered aircraft and carried a huge payload of bombs and ammo. Problem was, what good was an airplane like that now???

And wouldn't you know that the then popular general, Curtis Lemay, Commander of the Strategic Air would put in an order for new pilots for his Strategic Air Command, copilots of course. He had plenty of Aircraft Commanders. They were all recalls for the Korean War from WW2 and they had lots of flying hours and were old captains and majors trying to finish out their 20 years to retirement. This is what the young guys like Joe were facing when they finished training in 1955. Little did they know the seat end fate that awaited most of them.

It is only fitting to mention that one of Joe's good friends and fellow Cadets at Williams AFB in class 55M was a four star General-to-be and Chair of the Joint Chiefs of Staff, Larry Welch. Larry and Joe would keep in touch by proxy over the years to come.

Chapter 23

General Lemay's Air Force
(Strategic Air Command)

SO, FOLLOWING THE TRAINING into B26s along with many of those who had gone to multiengine training to begin with, off Joe went to the Strategic Air Command, or as it was commonly called in those days, "Lemay's Air Force." Lemay succeeded in making a dirty job out of what used to be fun for Joe and many other young pilots like him. So you say, "Well, you're getting paid aren't you? What's to gripe about?" Okay, I will tell you; do a better job of planning so the new guys know up front what is in store for them. Joe never saw a new young pilot in those days that wouldn't tell the same story. It was wrong of the Air Force to misrepresent what the plans were for these pilots. It was not uncommon to see younger pilots who were copilots who had never shot a landing or made a takeoff in a year since they got to the Strategic Air Command.

It was all about getting what they called "spot promotions" for the aircraft commander, who was the front seater, or the left seater as they were in those days. Many of the guys like Joe would have gone through the Air Guard if they had it to do over. At least you would have known what you were going to fly when you got back home to your Air Guard unit after training.

Joe was fortunate in one way though, he got to pick what part of the country he would go to for his service. When he was destined, that is to say sentenced, to SAC, he picked Davis-Monthan AFB in Tucson. That had become his second home when he met Mike Lipscomb.

Davis-Monthan AFB was home to the 43rd Bomb Wing and Air Refueling Squadron. Joe was assigned to the 43rd Refueling Squadron as a copilot.

Before he could check out as a copilot though it was necessary for him to attend the ground school for KC-97s at March AFB in Riverside, California. The school was a one month ground school designed to teach the operating systems of the KC-97s to new pilots.

THE MISSION OF THE KC-97 was to refuel the B-47 bombers, presumably on their way to their hostile targets. The object was then to rendezvous with the bombers at a predetermined point and to top off their tanks on the way to their targets. This would presumably give the bombers the added fuel they would need to hit their targets and fly back to friendly bases. So this was the way the Cold War was fought from a copilot's seat of the KC-97.

One Sunday while Joe was TDY, or temporary duty, to March AFB in Riverside, he decided he would drive up to Big Bear Lake to see what was going on in that part of the world. He had heard that Big Bear was sometimes the hang out of the rich and famous, and of the movie industry. He pulled up in front of the lodge, got out of the car, and walked up onto the porch of the main lodge when he noticed there was a volleyball game going on just to his right as he faced the lodge. He walked over to the edge of the porch to watch the game when he noticed this one clean cut guy with what you might say was a pretty body for a man. He had coal black hair and was dressed in a pair of athletic shorts. Joe thought to himself, "I've seen that guy before." And soon after, that guy made a great spike shot and a couple of other guys said, "Great shot Rock." Just bigger than life itself there was none other than Rock Hudson playing volleyball with the guys. There may have been other Hollywood greats out there on the court that day, but he was the only one Joe recognized for sure. Joe thought, "Well the world is sometimes a small place." Joe hung around the Lodge for an hour or so then made the trip back down the mountain towards Riverside.

Joe also met the base commander's daughter at the swimming pool the following day and that resulted in an invitation to have dinner with the Base Commander, his wife, and their daughter at the Commander's home that evening. Joe was impressed, but too old for that young lady, who was only seventeen at the time. Joe took his final exam the next morning and headed back to Tucson.

In the meantime, Mike Lipscomb had graduated from high school at age eighteen and being perhaps partially inspired by Joe, whom he deeply admired, decided to apply for admission to the 1st class of the new USAF Air Force Academy in Colorado Springs, Colorad,o to begin classes in August of 1955. Mike and Joe kept in touch, and Joe actually visited Mike in the spring of 1956. He had neat girls lined up for them, as always. Mike also came home to Tucson for all the holidays just to visit. And Joe was always welcome at the Lipscomb home.

Chapter 24

Newfoundland

THE AIR FORCE LEFT little time for Joe to linger though because the 43rd Air refueling squadron would soon be deployed to Earnest Harmon AFB, Newfoundland, in early December and not return until the first of March 1956. And wouldn't you know that the first night at Earnest Harmon AFB everyone went to the Officers' Club where the song playing on the juke box was "Sixteen Tons" by Tennessee Ernie Ford. Joe also spied, right away, the petite blonde sitting with a couple that was older. He would learn later that they were her older sister and brother-in-law. Her brother-in-law was a captain, but not a flying type. Joe asked her out the next evening and she accepted. Don't know how many of you have tried sex in a freezing car, but at that age, no one even paused to think. See she was eighteen and he was almost twenty-two. They went to the Officers' Club because that was the only nightlife on the base. Joe was able to find a car. Joe went to their home to visit, which was an apartment in the Officers' Quarters. Sometimes her sister and brother-in-law would go out and leave them there alone. They had great sex. It was very noticeable that she had one brown eye and one blue eye and one of her breast's was a little smaller than the other, though neither of them were small. Of course her sister was aware of what was going on and she obviously approved. They would sometimes get in bed as soon as sister and brother-in-law were out of sight.

Then before they hardly knew it, it was the first of March and the 43rd Air Refueling Squadron departed for Tucson. Joe told her he would be in touch, but he knew better when he said it. Joe was still on the move and deathly afraid of being too close to any woman. He subconsciously felt that his sex with the woman spoke for itself, but beyond that, it made his blood run cold.

Joe did take an occasional course at the University of Arizona and attended an occasional football game. He and one of his male friends were at a Saturday afternoon game and who would he run into? His love when he was in pilot training at Williams AFB, Janet Munch. She was just as pretty as ever and was with her boy friend, who was a PhD candidate in education. And boy, did she rip into Joe right then and there for putting her down. Joe just tried to play it down, and that was the last time he ever saw her.

Joe made $222.00 dollars a month plus $100.00 dollars flight pay for a grand total of $322.00 dollars. When Joe returned from B26 school, his old car had about had it so he went down and traded the old clunker on a new yellow Plymouth convertible with a white top. That was one cool car. Then he rented a two bedroom house near Speedway Boulevard. The car payment was $75.00 dollars a month and the rent on the house was $70.00 dollars a month. He had a good life outside.

It wasn't long until Joe received a call from his old friend from pilot training, Danny Lovell, who was returning to Tucson to fly for the Air Defense Command as an 86D interceptor pilot and he needed a place to stay. Since Joe had an extra bedroom, Danny just moved in with him.

Bob's Drive Inn was right around the corner from the house, and that was where all the muscle car guys hung out in the evenings. At the foot of Mt. Lemon there were two cattle guards which were exactly one half mile apart. It was common for the guys to debate who had the fastest car and sometimes they would even race for titles, that is, the loser had to give his car to the winner of the half mile race. And sometimes they just raced for bragging rights. It so happened that John had just bought himself a brand new Plymouth Fury which had a big block engine and was a very fast car. He did race against the local competition with Joe in the right seat and did win. They called it 'cattle guard to cattle guard'.

Chapter 25

Life At The Ranch

DANNY AND JOE WOULD live there for a couple of months. Then a couple of pilot friends of Danny's from the Air Defense Command on the other side of the field invited Danny to move in with them at what they would call The Ranch. It was a house located just off north 6th Avenue that sat on an acre of land with three bedrooms and a guest cottage and a swimming pool. It was a neat set up for a group of bachelors, so Joe agreed with Danny that the move would be a good idea. Joe and Danny did move to The Ranch, as it was called, and it was an absolute girl trap. They swarmed like flies on a cow's back or something like that. The Ranch was a lively place. It was to have been the retirement home for an elderly couple who lived in Kansas City. At some point they intended to fully retire there, but for now they leased it out.

This period in Joe's life also corresponded to a crisis that was going on with his family of origin. The cattle market had taken a turn for the very worst back home in Mississippi, as it had over the entire country. Joe's Dad had taken a big hit on his cattle, and he was panicked to liquidate. Joe's grandfather had told him to sit still, and everything would pan out for him if he was patient. But no he wasn't having it, and like a typical hot head, he sold out and moved to ElCentro, California, to go into the cattle feeding business with an old friend, Harold Dorsey, to whom he had shipped many loads of cattle before.

One of the guys that Joe lived with at The Ranch had bought an old Taylorcraft for $800 just to have a toy to fly around the local area. His name was Jason and he was a natural worrier, so they nicknamed him Mom. When

John and Joe moved to The Ranch, John chose to live in the main house and Joe chose the guest cottage. Joe likened The Ranch to one those old time fly catchers, the kind that had a sweet smelling sticky substance on a strip of paper, so that when the fly lit, its feet stuck to it, and he couldn't get away. Joe and his friends had many parties, and Joe laughed about renting the cottage out to the other guys during parties.

Joe had asked "Mom" if he could borrow the Taylorcraft one weekend to fly out to ElCentro to visit his parents. You have to know that Air Force or Navy pilot graduates had only to complete the necessary paper work in those days to get their commercial pilot's rating if they had an instrument rating. Anyway, "Mom" just tossed the keys to Joe and said, "See you when you get back." Joe loaded up with his razor, deodorant and an extra pair of Levi's and off to the airport he went. He threw his stuff in the airplane and checked the oil and fuel. They were both full, but there was no manual so he had no idea how far he could fly before he would need fuel. It was just him and a sectional map and a magnetic compass.

He taxied out to the end of the dirt strip, checked the mags and off he went. He had drawn a line on the map so he knew where he was. He had no idea how much fuel exactly was in the tank though. It only had an old style cork gage that floated on top of the fuel with a wire that stuck up through the fuel cap so the only way of knowing how much fuel was left was the length of wire sticking out of the fuel cap. By the time Joe got to Gilda Bend, which was almost half way, it appeared that he had used most of the tank of gas he started with. By his estimation he was bucking a headwind. The question was just how much. After getting by Gila Bend he flew on for another 15-20 minutes when he could see that he would shortly be out of gas. There were plowed fields and vegetation ahead so he knew this would be crop dusting country and just about the moment the little wire gage came to rest firmly on the fuel tank cap, indicating that he had no fuel left, he saw a short crop duster strip dead ahead at 12 o'clock. He put the nose down and pulled the throttle back and made a short base leg and landed .

There was no one home at the duster strip, but there was a bar and a service station/grocery across the road. Joe walked into the bar to find the owner of the crop dusting operation drinking beer with his friends. The owner offered him a beer but Joe said, "No thanks, but can I bum a little gas off you?"

The man's name was Duke and he stood up, shook Joe's hand and said, "Sure, I can spare you some gas." The two of them walked back across the road and proceeded to fuel the Taylorcraft. Joe thanked him for the fuel and Duke said, "Come on back anytime." Nice guy, thought Joe.

When Joe was on the climb out, back to 6000 feet, he wondered if he might sometime want to fly crop dusters; but he quickly decided that flying a duster would be a hot sweaty job unless you owned the company, and even then you would have to put up with alcoholic pilots that would keep the airplanes torn up, and from what he had heard the farmers were quick to complain about the dusters if they didn't make a good crop. But in their defense, you could never fly close enough to the ground and there was always that little spot that you missed.

The visit to ElCentro went well but Joe could tell that Dad was regretting the decision he had made to leave and cash out of much of what he had spent his life working for. He hadn't sold one of the farms, but the new place that he had bought in 1950 was gone, and here he was in the southern tip of California trying to fit his square peg into that round hole again, and Joe just thought he looked out of place. Joe and his Mom both knew Dad pretty well. The visit was short and when it was over, Joe hopped back in his borrowed aircraft and flew back to old Tucson without incident.

Joe would never forget one Saturday when a girl by the name of Barbara and Joe were there alone at The Ranch. Joe's trademark had always been that he was a great dancer. They danced until they were hot and sweaty and then they sat on the couch with a bottle of Tequila and plenty of lemon and decided they would just chug-a-lug the whole bottle. And this they did over about 30 minutes. What started out to be a love party was quickly turning into something else. This was not why he had invited her over. She was a good looking thing, and Joe had wanted to make love to her from the time they met a few months ago, but there had not been a convenient time until now. Suddenly, the bottle was empty and they decided that Joe should go to the liquor store and get another one. Joe did get to the liquor store and got another quart of Tequila, but unfortunately this was the rainy season and by the time Joe headed back to The Ranch there was a cloud burst. The rain was so hard that Joe could not see 50 feet in front of the car. He was speeding across Grant Road headed west when he realized the road came to a dead end. He slammed on the brakes and cut the steering wheel to the left. The car turned sideways and the passenger side wheels hit the curb. Later he would find that the front end would need to be realigned but otherwise he was lucky again. Joe always said he would rather be lucky than good any day. Joe did return to home only to find Barbara passed out on the couch. He laid down beside her, and they both had a nice nap. From then on he was careful about drinking too much Tequila because it can sneak up behind you and hammer you.

Chapter 26

Introduction to Dirt Bikes

JOE'S OTHER FRIEND, Rusty Sanders, who was also a copilot in the 43rd Refueling Squadron, decided that he would buy a new off road motorcycle. It was called the 1956 TR6 and was built by Triumph for the American market, particularly for the desert.

But never mind that, this was in the 50s when there still was a whiff of freedom left in the air. This bike came with knobby tires for off road and desert riding, but it had lights and was street legal. All you had to do to race it was pull the lights off and put number plates on. For those not acquainted, it was a vertical twin 650cc engine. It was the first dirt bike/road bike combination to be designed and built specifically for desert riding. And even with a girl on the back it would run 100 MPH. Rusty bought one and brought it by for Joe to see. Joe was still living at The Ranch at the time. It was a beautiful bike and along with the boredom of his now apparent death sentence to the right copilot seat in his flying job, motorcycling might be fun if you could go racing across the desert on that thing. It sort made his hair stand up a little when he saw that shiny new 1956 TR6. He did go looking at the bikes and found that BSA (British Small Arms) was building similar bikes. However, at the time they only had a 500cc single cylinder dirt bike called the Gold Star. BSA was soon to come out with their own 650cc twin called the Spit Fire. It had a different cam, and the engine had a slightly shorter stroke which made it a little faster on acceleration than the TR6. But for those who understand such stuff, the front end, that's the forks, of the TR6 were slightly raked forward making it handle better and more forgiving in a slide.

Chapter 27

Great Falls Montana and Lisa

THE 43RD AIR REFUELING Squadron was for sure a traveling squadron because in December of 1956 it would redeploy to the newly renamed Malmstrom AFB located just 6 miles east of Great Falls, Montana. They were told, in particular, to be sure to bring all their cold weather gear that included heavy coats, parkas, winter socks and head gear because the weather could be a stark contrast to the weather they were used to in Tucson and.

This base dated all the way back to 1941 when it became a training base for the US Army Air Corp. However, at that time, the base was located close to the town of Great Falls where the civil airport is now located. Within a short span of time the Army Air Force would move the base six miles to the east to its present location, and donate the base close to downtown to the city of Great Falls. This base has had a number of tenants including the Military Airlift Command and the Strategic Air Command and now is the home of USAF 341st Missile Wing and has been closed to all aircraft traffic except helicopters since 1996.

This base was previously named Great Falls AFB, but as in many cases, this base was renamed for a pilot who was killed in the crash of his aircraft on takeoff.

Colonel Einar Axel Malmstrom was killed when his T33 jet had an engine failure on takeoff, and he crashed just one mile off the runway in August 1954. He was well liked in the community, and they pushed for the USAF to rename the base in his honor. By history, he had been shot down over Germany on his 58th mission and held prisoner until the end of the WW2.

The Mission

THE PILOTS WERE TOLD that the purpose of the trip to Malstrom was to support a B47 bomber mission and to test the feasibility of launching an all out assault on the Soviet Union from the northwestern part of the United States direct. The B47s would come from various bases, mostly to the east, and the mission would be planned so that the tankers could launch out of Great Falls, Montana and fly to the end of the Aleutian Island chain off Alaska to the furthest most range of the tankers and then allow the B47s to penetrate the Soviet airspace to hit targets in the Soviet Union. This would stretch the mileage limits of the tankers and the B47s to the limit. The tankers would recover to Fairbanks , Alaska, and the bombers, after delivering the weapons, would fly toward the nearest friendly territory, and either land or eject from the aircraft where they could be picked up by friendly forces.

Joe's squadron departed Davis-Monthan AFB on 1 December 1956. The field elevation at Davis-Mothan AFB is 2680 feet. The computed flight time for the 800 mile flight was 3 hrs and 35 minutes. They would be landing at a slightly higher elevation of 3472 ft. The weather would be cooler and clear there so they could expect better performance from the aircraft engines because of the cooler air. The KC97 aircraft was powered by four Pratt and Whitney 4360 engines with a rated power of 3500 hp per engine. It had four rows of 7 cylinders.

They had a crew of eight per aircraft. After they landed and parked the aircraft, they unloaded all their luggage and were taken by bus to the barracks and officers' quarters. They were assigned rooms in close proximity to each other for ease of contact. The first thing on the agenda was to see when they had to brief for and plan their missions. It just happened to be Friday about 4 o'clock local time. They determined that their first work day would be Saturday morning where they had an initial briefing and flight planning for the first mission which would be flown Monday.

On the very first night in town, Joe met a young 2nd Lieutenant at the bar in the Officers' Club. He was slender and well muscled and like Joe he was a new, what they would call, 'slick winged pilot'. That was one who doesn't have a star or a star with a wreath around it to signify much more flying hours and almost a Devine Wizard of flying airplanes. So Joe knew they were on about the same experience level. And of course Joe was insanely jealous that this young guy was flying single engine jets while he was reading a checklist for another pilot. As the conversation progressed, his newly made acquaintance went on to say that he would be getting out of the service in the next few weeks. Joe asked why, and the guy said he just jumped out of an F84 last month, and he refused to fly them anymore. Joe chuckled and said, "Well maybe instead of quitting you should have told them to give you a better aircraft next time."And Joe thought, "I don't know about the future, but I've never been afraid in an airplane since my first solo flight." And he remembered well what a proud moment it was for him to do the required act after his first solo and stand on the table top in the cafeteria and while flapping his arms saying, " Today I soloed at 1530 hours, and I am now a full fledged bird man, USAF." Joe had never been afraid in an airplane since. He truly believed that his own mistakes and his mistakes alone would be the only thing that would ever kill him.

Oh, and like all units, they had their share of strange people. They had a Captain Senior Navigator who had taken up hypnosis, claiming that he, through hypnosis, could rid your life of all evils, real and potential. So he was going around doing hypnosis and he was doing it in groups and privately. So Joe asked if he could cure him of the need for wine and women and make it possible for him to just be a monk. Well, he tried, but it not only didn't work; it made the problem worse!

But to get back to the mission, Joe and the 43rd Air Refueling Squadron were there to participate in a large military exercise to determine the fitness and capability to refuel a large number of B47s coming through to hit targets inside the Soviet Union in the event of a necessary nuclear attack. This mission had to be done on a short notice basis to see if the concept of a massive nuclear attack was really feasible. There were several refueling squadrons participating in the event, all from different bases, with a total of 28 refueling tankers.

The plan was then for all 30 tankers to take off at one minute intervals, assume route formation, that is about 100 yards between tankers, then rendezvous with the B47's by ADF (Automatic Direction Finder) radio and VOR (Visual Omni Range). Between these two navigation aids, which the tankers had and also the bombers had , the tankers should be able to arrive just ahead of the B47 bombers and establish themselves in a holding pattern and as soon as the bombers were in sight, the tankers would come out of the holding pattern and establish themselves on a predetermined heading and altitude as the B47s approached from behind, or the six o'clock position. Once the bombers had the tankers in sight, they would simply close up the interval and get into position for hook up.

When the B47 was within about 50 feet, the **B47** pilot would open his receptacle door on the left side of the nose of the aircraft and move forward for contact. Meanwhile the boom operator on the tanker, who was an enlisted man, would lower his boom from the stored position and fly it into position with the small ruddervator of the boom. Once he was ready, he would direct the bomber pilot in terms of where to change his position until the bomber was in proper position. Once the bomber was in proper position, the boom operator would extend the several feet to make contact with the fuel receptacle of the bomber at which time the boom operator would transmit vocally, "Contact." The boom operator would then begin to transfer jet fuel (JP4) to the bomber. When the bomber had taken his allotted amount of fuel, either the boom operator or the B47 could initiate a disconnect.

An early photo of a USAF KC-97 refueling a B-47, similar to the hook-ups of the "Iron Bar" Operation. Photo: 8th RTS Lab, Tom Hildreth collection.

The tanker could off load up 40,000 lbs of jet fuel generally. The amount of off load was affected by how far out the tanker had to go to make the mission. In other words, the farther out in distance the tanker had to go to rendezvous with the bomber, the less fuel the tanker could off load. One must remember that the tanker used 115/145 gasoline for its engines, and the aircraft could only carry so much total weight. And the more aviation gas the tanker had to carry to get there and back for its own use, the less jet fuel it could carry to stay under the maximum weight for the tanker.

Piloting technique of the tanker was a bit tricky during the actual contact because the nose of the tanker would have a tendency to pitch down slightly on initial contact on the bomber with the boom of the tanker. The pilot of the tanker would have to hold a moderate amount of back pressure on the control yoke and then trim off the pressure and hold a steady platform. On the other hand, the bomber pilot had to make contact and then fly his aircraft so as to hold a steady constant position. And to do this, once he made a connection, the bomber pilot, or receiver as he was called , would have to add just a little power to hold his position while flying wings level. If all else was going well, the boom operator was at the same time transferring fuel. The most important thing for both pilots was to keep the pressure trimmed off the controls so that they are flying it with the tips of their fingers, and it was a teamwork situation all the way.

Now just let me say this, if you were a good formation pilot, this whole thing was a snap. If you're not, it was going to be a long day at the office. Pilots who had never flown single engine jets had the most problems. The bomber pilot and the boom operator and the tanker pilot all had to be on their A game for the operation to go smoothly. And there were a few tanker pilots who were downright panicked by the other aircraft being that close to the ass end of his aircraft. After all, the worst thing that could happen would be if you had a severe collision and all crashed and died. But if you think like that, you're in the wrong job. The good pilots would drive right up there, hook up, get his gas, and he was gone.

One of the factors discovered in the early going was that weather was an all too important factor in launching such a mission. Almost anyone can see that you couldn't launch a nuclear attack if the weather was bad. Without going into too much detail, can you imagine launching such an attack if there were clouds from the ground all the way up 30,000 feet? It would be impossible. What were they to do if the horn blew to launch and the weather would not permit them to launch? Were they to say, "Sorry, Mr. President, the weather is too bad to launch an attack." And this was the time when they had to rely on manned bombers.

Chapter 28

Great Falls

NOW TOMORROW WOULD be Friday and the weekend was, for the most part R&R, or rest and relaxation, while maintenance got the aircraft in shape to fly the missions they were sent there to perform. The first order of business for several of them, including Joe, was where was the food and entertainment. Some wanted to go to the Officers' Club; some wanted to hang out in the Officers' Quarters; and Joe and a couple of friends wanted to check out downtown Great Falls for food and entertainment.

So Joe and a couple of his friends were able to find that there was a nice restaurant downtown and also a nice piano bar near the restaurant. They checked with the motor pool and were able to get a car for the trip there and back. They all dressed in their best sport clothes, as was the custom at that time, picked up the car, and off they went to the city of Great Falls, only 6 miles away.

In those days Great Falls was a sleepy little town of maybe 10,000 – 15,000 population. Joe and his two friends arrived downtown at about 8 o'clock. The restaurant was the Barracuda Restaurant, and the piano bar was just across the street and about three doors down. They entered the restaurant, and there was a reservation line, but they still had a few seats left so they were seated right away. According to reports at the base, all their food was good, but their steaks and seafood were excellent. The waiter came shortly and appeared to be a sharply dressed young man about 30 years of age. He had dark hair, and he was thin and about 6 feet tall. He had on black trousers with a heavy crease, a white shirt and a black bow tie. He was very efficient, poured the ice water and laid out the menus. Joe's two friends were both single guys, like Joe. Paul was from Jonesboro, Arkansas, and Mickey was a product of Charleston, S.C. Both of them were also copilots on the KC97.

Soon the waiter returned for their orders. Paul ordered Red Snapper, and Mickey and Joe each ordered a ribeye steak, both cooked medium. They had all ordered tossed salads, and the waiter, whose name was Eric, returned shortly with the salads. The three of them talked about the coming mission they had been tasked to do and whether the weather would cooperate. It had looked 'iffy' the day before for the refueling long range forecast in the proposed refueling area. Time would tell. Soon Eric brought their salads, followed by the main course. Joe and Mickey said it was the best ribeye they had eaten in a long time, and Paul said the same for the Snapper. By 9 p.m. they were finished with their meal. They paid their checks and started walking toward the piano bar down the street. The temperature was a little chilly but each had on a heavy jacket which was sufficient.

They approached the bar and opened the door and entered. There were a number of tables and a good crowd was already gathering. There was a long bar on the left about 30 feet long and at the end of the bar there was the piano which was surrounded by stools on three sides, the other side joining the bar. There were about 10 stools at the bar. Some were occupied, but they were able to find three in a row so they could sit together.

There were already several of what Joe would call the main attraction, women, seated at the bar. Joe sat down next to one of them, as he would say back home, "the pick of the litter", and Paul, who like Joe, had a severe Southern drawl sat next to another one. The piano player was playing and singing "It Had To Be You" when they sat down. It turned out that this piano player could really bang out and sing a song. He was of medium build and about 50 years old. He had brownish blonde hair and said he had played with the Tommy Dorsey band years ago and other big bands but preferred a regular gig by himself at this point in his life. His name was Larry. He was a great musician and had a pleasant voice as well and a jar full of tips.

But the main attraction for Joe had become the redhead seated to his immediate left. Her name was Lisa, and she had a few freckles but had a pretty mouth, lips, teeth and nose. She told Joe that she lived just out of town to the Northeast. Actually she lived toward the base but with a left turn for about a mile when you got half way to the base. She was a legal secretary/paralegal by day and then a plaything at night, and she loved this particular piano bar. As far as Joe could tell, she was a GO. She had one child, a girl, who spent a lot of time with Lisa's mother when Lisa wanted a babysitter. Lisa was 5 feet 5 inches tall and weighed 105 pounds by his estimate. So Joe put his Southern charm to work, since she denied having a sweetie. He told her in the proper Southern drawl the he was just a good puppy from Mississippi who really didn't know much about this old world we live in and actually put on quite a need for sympathy act. He just flies them old airplanes around and barely gets by. Joe was quick to pickup on a weakness or soft spot when it came to women. Before long he'd have them wanting to kill for him. Anyway she took the bait. Now Joe didn't bring it on too hard, but he knew just how to work her. And before long he got her up on the dance floor, a small dance floor about 8x8 foot.

When they sat down, Lisa revealed more about herself. She was a smart student in school and loved to dance. She was twenty-three and had dated a lot of guys but ended up marrying her high school sweetheart. However, she thought at the time it was a mistake and learned from that experience that if you have a gut feeling about something like that, you'd better beware. She had finished college at the University of Montana in pre-law but had not yet decided whether to go ahead with law school. Was the time right? She had not yet answered that question in her own mind. Joe could not help but note those beautiful emerald eyes. This was one nice looking chick. He also had to admit that she was extraordinary in that she, so much like himself, was a deep thinker.

As the music played, they continued to talk and dance a few slow ones. Before they knew it, it was 11:30 p.m., and Mickey was saying they had a 0700 briefing and they, or at least he (sitting in the middle), was ready to get back to the base. Joe and Paul both agreed, but first Joe made plans with Lisa for the next night which was Saturday.

The Military has a way of controlling its people. And that way is by having you check in frequently, like with roll calls almost daily, except on some Sundays and occasionally on Saturday. They want to keep tabs on the troops, although this may vary from unit to unit depending on the CO (Commanding Officer). And at 0700 on Saturday, roll call was done with everyone in attendance. Lt. Col. Sanders was in charge of the exercise on which they were about to embark. He took the podium and said, "Gentleman, if you do not have a Top Secret clearance or if you know anyone in this room who does not have a Top Secret clearance, let it be known now."

He went on, "The mission here is twofold:

1) To test the limits of the Soviet Radar.

We will do this by penetrating as deep as possible into the Soviet Union without detection. In this flight the B47s will not be carrying a bomb. Our B47s are the new version, the B47F. It has newly designed Air Defense systems. This will be the acid test of whether it can make the target without detection by the Russian Radar. The details of the redesign are not available at this time. What we hope to gain from this experience is to convince the Soviet Union that they must come to the table so that we can all stop this senseless Cold War and spending ourselves out of existence as sovereign countries.

2) The second purpose of this mission will be to test structural changes to the B47 and to its engines and too check fuel consumption for the overall mission. We think the new Aircraft is up to the task, and we would not attempt this exercise if we didn't.

3) Now another important phase of this mission is to investigate the adequacy of the KC97 and its ability to put up the platform that the B47F needs for in-flight refueling. There is reason to believe that it is antiquated for the mission that is now demanded. This question is part of what we are here to evaluate. You will be given special log reports to be filled out on each mission, and you will do a debriefing when you return from the mission. And the results of your debriefing will be tallied and turned over to the Defense Department and will then be forwarded to the Armed Services Committee of the US House and Senate.

4) We will be flying proficiency missions over the local area for the next two weeks in order for all aircrews involved in this exercise to be at peak performance when the final test arrives.

5) The final test mission will be flown between 20 Dec and 25 December 1956.

6) This meeting will not be discussed outside this room. That is all. Meeting adjourned."

Joe was to call Lisa that evening about 5 p.m. He called her as she had asked. She said hello and Joe said, "I am free tonight, what shall we do?" She said, "How about a movie and then we go to the piano bar?" He said, "Count me in." She said, "Where can I pick you up?" He said, "Stop at the front gate. I will call and let them know to expect you. They will give you a visitor's pass and directions to the visiting officers' quarters. What time is the movie?" She said, "7 p.m., pick you up at 6:30." When she arrived, she was dressed in a black pants suit. As they were heading toward the main gate she said, "There is a new movie that has just come to town. The name of it is 'Giant'. Would you like to see it? You are aware of the death of James Dean, right? Rock Hudson took the role, and they have changed the story from the original oil field story to a different narrative all together. We will have to see what the new plot is." When Lisa and Joe arrived at the movie there was a line, so they had to go through the line and there were a few seats left when they found theirs. As it turned out, the story had completely changed from the original intent, and Lisa and Joe were disappointed in the redo of the movie, but it was worth seeing.

The movie theatre was only two blocks from downtown, but the temperature was about 45 F. She parked on the street about 100 feet away from the bar. Once seated at the piano bar she said, "I didn't know if you would call." He said, " I didn't either. I am afraid of how I may appear rather shy when it comes to intimacy." She said, "Yes, I think I know where you're coming from." Then Joe tipped the piano player, and he began to play and sing "As Time Goes By". Lisa said, "Remember 'Casa Blanca'?" And Joe said, "Yes, I've seen it, but when it came out, I was too young to appreciate it." Lisa said, "Me too, but isn't it a beautiful song?" They both agreed as they were dancing.

Joe just wanted to spend the whole night with Lisa. She was different from all the women he had ever known. She was educated and beautiful. They danced to more of the oldies and by the time the piano bar closed at 1:00 am, they knew each other's history completely, well almost completely. There was still that little part of a Joe that was deeply afraid of complete commitment.

As they pulled away from the bar Lisa said, "Do you want to go to the Officers' Quarters or would you like to stay at my house tonight?" Joe quickly responded, "Sure, we can go to your place." On the way to her place Joe said, "I'm lucky we don't have a Sunday schedule this week." On the way home, which was only about four miles from town and in a nice neighborhood, Lisa said, "Lee Ann, my daughter, is spending the night with her Aunt Lillian."

She also shared that she had married her high school sweetheart after just one year of college, but the marriage was a casualty of being in an unhealthy groove for a long time. However, before she could apply for an annulment, she was pregnant. Soon after Lee Ann was born, she sued for and got the annulment because she didn't want to have to deal with him over the child. By now they were pulling up in the driveway and into the garage. She closed the garage door and then opened the door to the house where it was toasty warm. Joe felt at home. Lisa went on to say that her Dad was an attorney and senior partner in the largest law group in town. She was employed as a paralegal at the firm.

She and Joe sat down on the sofa in the living room. Then she said, "Are you hungry or would you like some coffee?" Joe said, "No thanks, I'm not hungry or thirsty." They started kissing on the couch and then she said, "Shall we retire?" Of course Joe said, "Yes."

Lisa turned on the bedside lamp as she removed her clothes while he was doing the same. He knew just at the moment she removed her pants that she was a true redhead, and he didn't think that he had ever gazed upon a more beautiful body in his life. If there ever was a better looking specimen, he didn't remember it. And she appeared to be equally pleased with what she saw. They crawled in between the covers. Their lovemaking was true and passionate. They both experienced the most complete match of lovemaking Joe had ever experienced. He simply could not ask for more. He had always heard that redheads were better lovers. Now he knew.

Finally, they awakened about 8:30 am. They talked for a long time before getting out of bed. Joe felt that for the first time in his life he finally had someone who shared the same values and aspirations that he had. "This is the one!" he said to himself. They lay in bed just talking about anything and everything. He told her about all his fears where women were concerned, and his basic distrust of women. He also told her about all the torrid love affairs that he had previously and that he wasn't certain of the reason but that he did not feel the same with her. And for whatever the reason, he did not feel defensive with her. Lisa said she understood and he need never feel pressured by her. If he needed space just tell her.

He also told her about his love/hate relationship with the USAF and how he felt like the Air Force and General Lemay had betrayed him and not kept their side of the bargain after he signed up. He thought he had signed up to fly fighter jets only to be relegated to the copilot seat of a refueling tanker. There must be a better way. Lisa said she could see that he had been deeply hurt and perhaps there was something better out there for him.

In the meantime, with Joe sitting at the breakfast table, she cooked scrambled eggs, bacon and biscuits and gravy that were just out of this world. Joe just wasn't believing the multilevel of talents and psychic insights of this woman. Joe told Lisa about his attraction to motorcycles and about his racing and his wild escapades on the bikes. She looked at him smiling and said, "Oh, I already figured you to be the 'smash-mouth' type, and I admire that trait about you." He thought to himself, "She's the only one who has ever really understood me."

He told her as much about their mission as he could and said that if all went off as planned, he would be leaving about the 23rd of December, headed back to Davis-Monthan AFB in Tucson. She immediately asked if he could return to see her in the spring. She said she loved hiking and fly fishing for trout. Lisa said, "I only like to catch and release though. I am not a meat hunter or fisherman." He said he would try to take some leave time in April to visit, and she was ecstatic. In the meantime, he hoped to see her regularly over the next two and one-half weeks.

Meanwhile, there were actually four squadrons participating in the events at the base. Each squadron would fly four sorties each per day to gain the necessary proficiency to refuel twenty-eight B47Fs off the Aleutian Islands headed west to test the Russian radar and to try out the performance of the new B47F and Air defense systems aboard the aircraft, including the new Stealth system that was in the experimental stages. If it tested out positively then the Air Force would request the whole B47E inventory be modified to the B47F model thus it would not be necessary for the Air Force to buy as many of the new B52s that would soon be appearing off the assembly line.

The next day, Monday, would be the first encounter of the B47F, and Joe was on board for one of those flights. The new model had speed brakes on it which allowed the pilot to slow the aircraft fairly rapidly and then retract the speed brakes and then lower the wing flaps to 1/4 flap setting, which had the effect of making the aircraft more stable at a tanker speed of 190 knots indicated airspeed. This was about as fast as the KC97 would fly at METO power or max continuous power. It also had afterburners on the four inboard engines for use, if necessary to get out of harms way. This aircraft, with full power and four after burners, had a max speed of 1.35 Mach, which was faster than any aircraft the Soviets had, including the MIG 29. The only problem was the additional fuel. Thus you could only use afterburners for a limited few minutes without compromising the range for the aircraft. You could only use full power for a short period without running the aircraft out of fuel. The cruise speed though was 580 knots true airspeed for max cruise flight.

During the training sessions one of the KC97s broke a propeller blade on its number 2 engine, which went through the fuselage and damaged the aircraft, but the aircraft did not catch fire or explode, and the crew was able to make a three engine landing after dumping all its jet fuel. This occurred soon after takeoff, so it was a hurry up and dump fuel so the crew could get the aircraft back on the ground safely. Breaking and throwing a prop blade was always a hazard when taking off in a heavily loaded KC97. The pilots were always careful to look for cracks in the prop blades on their preflight.

Also one aircraft lost power just before liftoff during a practice mission and did hit the cable barrier at the end of the runway. A total of forty practice sorties were run over the next two weeks leading up to the final test on 22 Dec 1956, and at the end all systems appeared to be GO.

The completion of these exercises led up to December 22, 1956, which was the day of exercise TANGO. On the morning of December 22 at 0600 hrs. the briefing began. Lt. Col. Sanders started the briefing of the route and rendezvous times and any special instructions. When he was finished they had the weather briefing. The visibility was good that day and that was a plus. There were scattered to broken clouds with tops at 3000 ft . They got their time hack.

Lt. Col. Sanders revealed at this time the particulars of the B47F mission; that is, that they would penetrate 1000 miles into Soviet air space deep into Siberia and then turn back home and recover at the Elmendorf AFB base in Anchorage, Alaska. This base had a full complement of facilities necessary for recovery of large jet aircraft. This mission was so important in that it not only would evaluate US capabilities and the modified B47F but also and most importantly, the capability of the Russian defense.[1] They were to fly down the Aleutian chain and hit their holding point. Then they would tune in the radios to the rendezvous frequency and get in the holding pattern and wait, but before they could make one trip around the pattern, the twenty-eight bombers were eight miles out. The tankers leveled out on a heading straight toward Siberia and things were happening at a fast pace. The B47Fs were upon them and within ten minutes each B47F had topped off their tanks with 40,000 pounds of JP4 jet fuel, all without incident, and they were on their way to Siberia. Meanwhile, the tankers turned and picked up a new heading for Fairbanks, Eielson AFB, just twenty-six miles southeast of Fairbanks, which is 105 miles from the Arctic Circle.

The B47F recovery plan was to return to Elmendorf AFB at Anchorage, Alaska, once they had flown into Siberia 1000 miles to their particular target, for example Moscow or Leningrad, or if, or when, they detected hostile activity, or had been discovered. Elmendorf AFB is a large facility with runways running North/South and East/West and long enough to handle the larger jet aircraft. If the base was rated by stars, it would be a five star base.

All that practice for two weeks paid off. Everything had been done without mistake or mishap on the launch of exercise TANGO. The recovery of the tankers to Eielson AFB, near Fairbanks was without incident.

The B47F part of the mission was a little different. The new Stealth feature which was being tested was effective until the B47Fs were 800 miles deep into Russian territory. Then they received electronic evidence that they had been detected. All of them made 180 degree turns for home and pushed their power up to 100% without afterburners. They had special aft looking radar for the express purpose of picking up enemy interceptor aircraft. They would save the afterburners just in case some enemy interceptor aircraft might be detected to be gaining on them. The longer they could fly without using the afterburners, the better chance they had of not running short on fuel.

At 100% power their ground speed was 590 knots, just shy of the speed of sound. If they had to they could go into afterburner and reach a speed of 1.3 Mach, which would put them beyond the speed of any Russian fighter. All the B47F aircraft recovered to Elmendorf AFB, Alaska. Once they were out of range of Russian fighter jets, they called Elmendorf tower and began to pick up spacing in flights of four, the lead flights maintaining 100% power and the trailing flights pulling their power back slightly to pick up spacing for landing and at 150 miles out they would start a gradual descent for landing and continue to pick up spacing for landing. The landing facility was prepared for their arrival but only given 30 minutes notice and told to clear all traffic for the incoming landing.

Meanwhile, the KC97s had all landed at Eielson AFB near Fairbanks Alaska. They refueled and turned the flights around and flew directly back to Malmstrom AFB at Great Falls, Montana, and landed. As soon as they were debriefed and turned loose, Joe called Lisa. She said, "Oh, I always love to hear your voice." He said, "Its mutual. What time are we on for and what are our plans?" She said, "We'll talk about that when I pick you up about 5:30 alright?" He said, "You're on. See you then, bye." Joe then called the front gate and told the airman to be looking for her and to issue her a pass.

It was about two o'clock now, so Joe could lounge around for a couple of hours and take a nap. It had been a long day. By the time he awakened it was about 3:30. He still had on his flying suit. He later walked into the lobby area and found Paul seated in one of the lounge chares. Joe asked if Paul's part of the mission went well, and Paul answered, "Yes, ours went well. How about yours?" Joe responded that they had a bit of a prop overspread on number one engine on the first takeoff. But the flight engineer handled it alright by reducing the throttle setting. So they had to watch that engine carefully throughout the rest of the mission. By now they had heard that all the B47Fs got back okay and that they had penetrated deep into the Russian defenses.

Paul finally got around to asking "How is your newest love life?" Joe said, "I don't know for sure yet. Either I am totally infatuated with Lisa, or I have found my true love after all this time, and I really think it is the latter because I have never before had such an intense feeling about a girl. She is the most heady woman I have ever seen. I have not seen even one wrinkle in her demeanor. So honestly, I am totally confused. When I am with her, the whole rest of the world is on hold." Paul laughed and said, "This one sounds different." Joe said, "Different for sure. I'm not counting any chickens just now. I've had intense feelings before but I have never before thought that the girl really understood me completely. It's like we both are at the same place at the same time in history." Paul said, "Are you planning to see her again? You know we leave tomorrow for home." Joe said, "We'll talk tonight. She is picking me up at 5:30."

Joe got in the shower about 4:30 and after his shower he realized that Lisa had not said what the plans for the evening were. So, just to be sure, he put on a white shirt, a tie and his best sport coat. He finished dressing by 5:15 and just for good measure he put on a spray of that cologne that she said she liked the first night they had met. It was 'Inspiration' by Lauder. He was sitting in the lounge near the front when she arrived, as advertised, at 5:29 by his time.

He walked to the car, opened the door and got in and said, "My, you are punctual." She said, "Yes, my father taught me." As they were driving out the gate he said, "What's on for tonight?" She said, "I'm taking you to a resort not too far from here at Black Eagle. I haven't been there for a while, but I have called, and they are open this evening." Then she was pulling over to the curb and when stopped she said, "I'm tired of doing all the driving. If you can fly an airplane at the speed of sound, you should be able to drive us to the lodge." Joe opened the door and went around to the other side and got into the driver's seat, and off they went. She moved over close to him and allowed her hand to rest on his leg. It was really a simple route out of town on one of the main roads and then right on to the resort. She went on to say, as he was driving, that they had a nice dining room and a combo playing the music. "They also have rooms if we elect to stay, but what time is your show to fly back to Tucson?" He said, "0900 hours." She said, "That's good. We can leave tonight, or we can return in the morning."

They drove on for about ten minutes, and Lisa told him that the Black Eagle Resort was coming up soon. It was near the road they were on. Soon they saw the sign, turned and pulled up into parking lot. It was a beautiful lodge with the looks of winter cabin in the mountains but much larger, a rustic appearance of a dark wooden log outer structure and a porta-cochere where Joe pulled up and stopped underneath. He would let Lisa out and then park the car. He met her inside. They had checked the weather before coming to be sure that no bad weather was in store for this evening or the morning.

Lisa had made reservations earlier so they were able to proceed directly into the dining area and be seated.

The dining room, like the outside, was one of rustic appearance with old but comfortable western chairs. They were seated by the hostess. There was a large fireplace with a fire burning with real wood. The waiter appeared shortly with water and menus. The waiter introduced himself as Hunter, after which he explained the menu options. Hunter was about 5 feet 8 inches tall and about 150 pounds. He appeared to be Latino but had a normal American voice. He had a short mustache and a chin beard only. He was very pleasant and accommodating. Joe and Lisa looked at the menu briefly, and Lisa selected the broiled pheasant, while Joe selected the prime rib, medium. Lisa said, "Do you always order your meat medium?" Joe answered that he used to order it medium rare until he learned that medium rare is actually harder for the GI tract to digest, and you are much more likely to contract a disease from it when you eat it that way. The meat must be at 149 degrees F for twenty minutes to kill all bacteria and parasites. Lisa said, "It's strange that you would have that much insight." Joe said, "I've always had an interest in things medical, I don't know why."

Before twenty-five minutes had gone by, they were served. They both had Caesar salads followed by their entrees. After a few minutes, Lisa remarked that her pheasant was delightful. Joe said his prime rib was as good as advertised as well. They also had a bottle of red wine made from Black Spanish grapes. Joe looked at the bottle label and noted that this wine had been fermented by the Sleepy Hollow Winery at Baldwyn, Mississippi. Joe said, "What a strange coincidence. That's about 150 miles north of where I was born and raised." By now Joe had decided that they would stay the night here since they would have plenty of time to get up in the morning and make it back to the base in time for him to pack his stuff for the trip. And he knew if they slept at her house, she would insist on making breakfast for him, and he didn't want her have to go to all that trouble. Actually, he had been careful not to scatter things around before he left the barracks so that it would be easy to pack when he got back in the morning. Lisa said, "I will pay the check." And Joe said, "Not on your life. I'm paying for this trip." Joe paid the check and said, "Lets stop by the desk on the way into the bar and reserved a room."

They went into the bar and noted that there were tables, booths and places at the bar. It was just 8:15, and the band was already playing. They took a booth for more privacy and ordered wine since they liked the wine they had in the dining room. After they had danced several times and Joe had showed off his dance skills, they sat in the booth and talked for a while. He could not help but notice that she was easy to talk to and he was saying things to her that he had never shared with anyone before, such as family relationships or lack thereof. She was a good listener and didn't appear to react negatively to his honest feelings about the world, people and family. She listened patiently and did not have a judgemental or condemning bone in her body.

Then it was her turn to share . She was an only child. Her parents wanted more children, but they just never happened, so she was an only child, not by choice but by circumstance. She was loved by both her mother and her father, but you might say she was a Daddy's girl too. Her mother had died 5 years ago of breast cancer, and she thought that could have had something to do with her early marriage to her old high school boyfriend. Nonetheless, her Dad had stuck with her through bad times and never wavered. She did have a paralegal degree from the University of Montana, but just had not, up to this time, gone on and finished a law degree. It was not that she didn't like law as a profession, she was just procrastinating about it. "I think I will do it at some point, I just haven't decided when." She went on, "My Dad and I are close, but he doesn't butt into my business unless I ask. I suppose my Dad would remarry, but he's not the chasing type. He is comfortable in his own skin, and there has been no one that he was interested in. He was comfortable with my mother. It took some adjustment, but he is perfectly comfortable with who he is and where he is. He is the perfect example of a man as I see it. He is accepting of the world around him on its terms." Joe said, "That's a great man. I hope I have the privilege of meeting him some time." Lisa said, "I have traveled the world over with my parents to Europe, England, France, Italy, Japan, Singapore, you name it."

Joe said, "All my travel has been for Uncle Sam at his expense to Newfoundland, Texas, Alaska, Oklahoma, Arizona, California, and Montana." Then Joe asked her to dance again. He showed her the East Coast Swing, the Twist and the Bop, and she was impressed, to say the least. Joe saw himself falling hopelessly in love. She had all the character, the looks , the manners and education that he could ever want. She was totally different from anyone he had ever known before. They went upstairs to their room , showered and went to bed and too soon it was 0630 in the morning.

The next mourning Joe and Lisa were already awake at 0615 and getting dressed so that she could take him back to the base. They finished dressing, went downstairs, where Joe paid the hotel bill, and they headed for the car.

Lisa said, "You drive to the base." Joe agreed, and off they went. On the way they discussed future plans. Joe said that he had some leave time that he could take in April, maybe between the 1st and the 15th. If that was agreeable, he would take the leave and they could do some hiking and fly fishing (catch and release) because he was neither a meat hunter or fisherman. Lisa said, "I'm glad to hear that because I am the same way. I love to catch them, but I don't want to kill anything either. Let's plan on it, weather permitting. And if we have inclement weather during that time period, we will find something else to do. We might even fly to Seattle or San Francisco. We'll just let the weather at the time dictate our plans."

As they approached the base gate Joe stopped, showed his ID card and the airman gave him a visitor's pass and saluted. Joe returned the salute. When they came to the Officers' Quarters, a short distance away, Joe pulled along the curb and stopped the car. Lisa got out and helped him carry his belongings inside and then they returned to the car. They hugged, kissed and said goodbye, but just for the moment. Joe said, "I will call when I reach Tucson." He saw that she had tears in her eyes as he squeezed her hand and walked away.

Chapter 29

Back to Tucson and Work

NOW IT WAS BACK TO business, but it wasn't quite the same and he knew it. But he did what he had always done and started trying to put her out of his mind. It was back to the business of flying now. He quickly packed his gear and his clothes and made his way to the lobby. He was greeted by Paul, Mickey and some of the other guys saying, "Well did you score or did you take a heavy hit?" They were trying to be funny. Joe said, "A little bit of both, but mostly the latter."

In a few moments the bus was there to take them to the briefing room. It was about a one minute trip, but they continued on out to the aircraft to unload their baggage, after which the bus took them back to the briefing room. They all got out and proceeded into the building and into the briefing room. It was now 0850 hours, so they all assumed their proper seats according to aircrew and momentarily Lt. Col. Sanders approached the room, and the room was called to attention, followed by, an at ease gentlemen command. The Lt. Col's comments were brief, saying that overall their mission had been a great success, and that all aircraft were recovered successfully. Much was learned from the mission, especially for a mission of that magnitude. The results had been passed up the chain of command for evaluation purposes. He then covered the details of the departure, following which the aircrews departed for their individual air craft.

Joe and his aircraft Commander, Major Randy Wilson, and their crew performed the preflight for the aircraft as usual and found no discrepancies that would significantly hamper their flight home. They would be in a flight of four KC97s, and they would be the number three of four aircraft. They connected auxiliary power to the aircraft after loading all gear aboard and checked in on ground control frequency and got the heads up to start engines. With all engines running, the loadmaster pulled the chocks and came aboard, closing and locking the door behind him. The aircraft was ready to taxi. All four aircraft checked in, and the number one aircraft told the flight to go taxi frequency and check in. They did that, and after the lead aircraft was in touch with the tower, they taxied out in order. Joe was handling the communications, as did other copilots. They taxied down the long taxiway to the approach end of the runway. They were using the North-South runway and were taking off to the South. Joe had read all the checklist down to and including the Before Take Off checklist, and they were number three for the active runway to the South (Runway18). They would take off at one minute intervals, as briefed, and stay in route formation for their flight back to Tucson, Davis-Monthan AFB. Flight time was about 3 hours and 30 minutes. The weather was clear, and they flew at 11,000 feet.

The flight home to Tucson was a bore. When they got to the parking area and with chocks secured, the loadmaster opened the door, they could see there was a crowd of family members beyond the fence in the parking lot awaiting their loved ones. As for Joe, he just needed to get his bags and head for his pad.

Back at the base it was always the same old drag. In addition to riding shotgun on the air refueling missions it was the copilot's job to bring everyone's flight lunches. Joe only had one friend in the squadron and that was another copilot by the name of Rusty Sanders. Rusty had graduated from pilot training about the same time that Joe had but had graduated from multiengine school. By now they were both totally bored with General Lemay's Air Force.

The unit was resuming its normal home training missions. They had proven with the Montana trip that they could perform the mission with which they were tasked without significant flaw. Also the new version of the B47, the F model, had performed exceptionally well, being able to penetrate the Soviet radar and get out. Of course this whole matter was causing an international raucous, but that would soon pass.

The pilots were now at early morning briefing for flying a practice mission. The unit was flying two sorties this morning, Joe's crew and one other.

Joe's aircraft commander was "Dad" Burk, who was forty-three already and was one of those older WW2 types who had been recalled for Korea and now was hoping to sweat out his retirement. He and his wife were Joe's best friends, and they were like surrogate parents to Joe. They were from Virginia.

The crew did get their briefing. It was a practice refueling flight. The rendezvous point was to be 120 nm out the 045 degree radial of the Tucson VOR (Visual Omni Range) which would intersect a radial of the Albuquerque VOR. They got the weather briefing and a time hack. They were to rendezvous and refuel on a heading of 270 degrees at 12,000 feet. The two aircraft would taxi out in formation and depart at tone minute intervals. The mission was simple and there were no questions. The crews departed the briefing room for the aircraft.

The two aircraft were in close proximity to each other on the ramp so it was a easy to communicate with each other during preflight. Both aircraft checked out okay on the ground, so both crews got into their respective aircraft and checked in on ground channel, following which they started engines. Then they went to tower ground channel for taxi instructions. Once at the end of the active runway, which today was to the southeast, they did their pre takeoff checks and went to primary tower and asked for takeoff. The tower responded, "Cleared for takeoff runway 12, the winds 140 at 10, altimeter setting 2996." The two KC97s taxied into position on the runway with Joe's aircraft in the lead position. They released brakes and ran the power up to max power, after which the engineer said all engines looked good. So they were on the roll and one minute later Number 2 released his brakes and the flight of two was off and running. By now the first flight was raising its gear and it held a straight heading until it reached 1000 feet, and then started a slow left turn. The number two aircraft started a left turn and joined up off the left wing. By now they were east of Tucson and climbing to intercept the 045 degree radio of the Tucson VOR. Number 2 was now joined up on the left wing, but was told to take the right wing, which he did. They were each carrying 20,000 pounds of JP4 jet fuel for offload to the two B47s and they were now passing through 4,000 feet and climbing to 12,000 feet. They had been passed to Tucson approach control and finally to Albuquerque Center. They reached the rendezvous point and established a holding pattern on a heading of 300 degrees. About that time the B47s were within 10 miles and after one loop around the holding pattern the two tankers departed on a heading of 300. The bombers already had visual contact at one mile and skies were clear in the refueling area, as had been predicted in the weather briefing.

The 1st B47 was approaching and was to hook up with Joe's tanker for refueling and had an instructor pilot in the back seat and a new pilot in the front seat for his first ride. At the first attempt the receiver (B47) was too fast and went underneath the tanker towards the front. Joe saw him as he shot underneath in front of the tanker. The pilot of the bomber backed off on the power and got in the trail position again for another shot. This time he hit the refueling boom but jerked the power off and went 50 feet below. On the third attempt, he hit the refueling boom as he was coming up and snatched his aircraft upward striking the boom and hitting the horizontal stabilizer of the tanker. There was a notable hard bump followed by the nose of the tanker pitching down and then violently up and it took both pilots on the controls to keep it from stalling. It lost airspeed rapidly. They could barely keep the aircraft flying above stall speed. The aircraft commander ordered the engineer to dump the jet fuel immediately, which he did, and Joe declared an emergency to Albuquerque Center and a vector to the Davis-Monthan AFB. They were about 80 miles out. They called a Mayday, or emergency, and put the IFF on Emergency code.

But the immediate problem was not getting home, it was whether or not Joe and Major Burk could now control the aircraft well enough to return it to the base. They were dumping fuel as fast as they could while they were turning to a heading towards Tucson. With both pilots on the controls, they were fighting to keep the nose down while losing airspeed. Their flying suits were both ringing wet with sweat. Major Burt, after consulting with Joe, did not think they could control the upward pitch of the aircraft long enough to get it back to base so the aircraft Commander ordered the crew to prepare for bailout. The trim was in full nose down. The collision had damaged the elevator of the tanker making it impossible to continue controlled flight.

Meanwhile, they had lost about 3,000 feet and were barely above stall speed. They were nearing necessary bailout altitude, and they were still 60 miles from home and there were no other airports nearby where they could safely land the aircraft. The best Joe and the aircraft Commander could do was a controlled descent at about 500 feet per minute. They did some quick mental calculation and concluded that they would never be able to nurse this thing that far. They were losing altitude too fast. The terrain around this area was 3,500-4,000 feet elevation and they were passing through 8,000 feet when the aircraft Commander and Joe agreed that they must get out of the aircraft.

The aircraft Commander notified the crew by interphone that he would be ringing the bailout bell shortly. Then after the crew was all out of the aircraft, he and Joe would release the controls and bailout behind them. The loadmaster had opened the doors, and the crew was standing by. The Commander rang the bell, and all the crew bailed out; then he and Joe, with all the down trim rolled in, let the yoke go and moved as fast as possible for the exit. As Joe bailed out he saw that all the other crew members had good chutes.

The Emergency was heard by Air traffic Control and Davis-Monthan, who promptly dispatched Emergency Helicopters to the scene. The crew members all landed close together, except for the two pilots who were found about a mile and a half away. There were a few scrapes and scratches but no serious injuries. When the helicopters returned to Davis-Monthan, the crew went straight to the base hospital for evaluation of all injuries. After treating all the minor injuries, the whole crew was returned to operations for debriefing where they also found that the B47 involved in the accident had sustained a large dent to the left side of the nose and that they had to cut the hole open to extricate the Navigator. The navigator was, however, not injured.

One thing that Joe did learn on this flight though was that the copilot **was** an indispensable member of this crew and without his help and muscle on the flight controls this would have been the final and disastrous flight for this whole crew.

About two weeks later Joe was scheduled to fly with the Commanding Officer of the Air Refueling Squadron, Lt. Col. Jerry O. Sprayberry. The CO had wanted to practice some instrument flying in the local area along with some instrument approaches. Lt. Col. Sprayberry was a nice man. He was about 50 years old and was another Korean War recall. A nicer officer Joe had never met. His face was wrinkled, and his hair was short and almost all gray. He was a short man, about 5 feet 7 inches tall, and weighed about 150 pounds. The Lt. Col. attended the flight briefing and outlined the flight he wanted to accomplish. There would be several extra flight members along as extra crew who were on the flight to log flight time. Joe and the Lt. Col. were the only pilots. They would sort of alternate being under the hood, so to speak, and that way both of them would get some hood time. It was to be a four hour local area flight . Sprayberry would take off and proceed out to the local instrument area and practice some basic maneuvers like timed turns and climbing turns and then they would return to the base and shoot some instrument approaches. They would then get approach control to vector them to the VOR and GCA (Visual Omni Range and Ground Controlled Radar) approaches.

Lt. Col. Sprayberry flew the take off and asked Joe to get a radar vector to the practice instrument area. This Joe did and when in the practice area Lt. Col. Sprayberry began by making some level turns and they monitored approach control frequency so they could keep themselves advised of local traffic. After that he gave the airplane to Joe and said , "I want you to start on this heading, south and give me a 3 degree per second turn to the right at 500 feet per minute climb." Joe said to himself, "Please sir, don't throw this rabbit in that briar patch." But Joe nailed it, and the colonel said, "I didn't know you could do that!"

They did some more basics, and then Joe asked approach control for a vector and a GCA approach. Approach control did vector them, and Lt. Col. Sprayberry shot a GCA final that was an okay approach, as Joe saw it. Then on the go around he told Joe to take the aircraft and to shoot one himself. Joe shook the yoke and said, "I got it." He called for the power settings, but on the downwind leg he said to the engineer, "I have the power." Then Joe, under radar vector, shot his version of a GCA approach, and when he pulled up off the approach the Lt. Col. Said, "Mercy boy, I did not think you could do that." "Thank you sir!" Joe replied excitedly.

They kept shooting approaches until they had shot 6 GCA's and then Sprayberry asked Joe to get them a vector for a VOR approach which he would shoot. When they were on the go around, Sprayberry suddenly slumped over the yoke, and the aircraft headed nose down for the ground. Joe grabbed the yoke and yelled at the Navigator, who was standing nearby, for help. The Navigator grabbed the Lt. Col., loosened his seat belt and with the help of a couple of other crew members pulled him out of the seat and began to do CPR on him as Joe notified the tower that they were in closed traffic and needed an ambulance to meet them at the end of the runway. Joe executed the traffic pattern and made a perfect landing , pulled the aircraft off the runway, steering it with brakes only, and shut it down as soon as he was in a place where he was not blocking traffic.

The ambulance was there within one minute to take Lt. Col. Sprayberry to the hospital. The doctors at the hospital said that Sprayberry had had a heart attack and was in the ICU and in stable condition. Joe was terribly concerned but happy that he had been able to do his part in bringing his friend home safely.

Chapter 30

Great Falls or Bust

JOE APPLIED FOR TWO weeks leave in early April to go to Montana to visit Lisa. When he called her, she was absolutely thrilled and said maybe they could go to the mountains if they had nice weather.

The last week in March, Joe began to lay out the things he would take to Montana with him. The main things he would take would be plenty of Levi's and shirts for outdoor wear. He would take his long underwear too in case of cold weather, along with his military boots for hiking and maybe two dress outfits, ties and plenty of socks. He had decided to drive, and it would take two days to get there. He wanted to see some of the country that so far he had not had the opportunity to see, except from the air.

Joe left Tucson on April 1st and headed first for Phoenix, then Flagstaff, Salt Lake City and then straight north to Idaho Falls, Butte, and on to Great Falls, Montana. He drove through Casa Grande and Phoenix then headed for Flagstaff. He thought the whole countryside was magnificent the way it gradually changed from desert in the lower elevations to high desert as he went along. He was maybe 50 or 60 miles north of Phoenix when he saw the Cottonwood, Arizona exit coming up on the left. As he rounded a slight bend and drove up a hill in the road he suddenly noticed that a car, a station wagon, was upside down in the middle of the road. There was no other traffic on the road at the moment, so he was the first one at the accident scene. He quickly pulled off the road, stopped and ran to the car and as he knelt down he could see that a man was the only occupant. The man was lying on his back, still breathing, but was gurgling fluid which he had aspirated from his stomach. Joe knew that time was not on his side, and he remembered what he had learned from his emergency training in the Air Force. He knew that he could have a fractured neck, but he also knew that he was strangling from the aspirated stomach content and that that could kill him even quicker.

Joe carefully slid him out onto the asphalt on his back and began cardiac compressions, five in a row and then oral respiration's by mouth. By then another car arrived, and Joe asked that he go find a place to call an ambulance. Within 5 minutes the Highway Patrol was there, followed a couple of minutes later by an ambulance. (What was an ambulance in those days? It was like a funeral hearse in which one could not stand erect). Joe got in the ambulance and performed CPR on this man all the way to the Cottonwood hospital. The man did not live, but none the less Joe and his commanding officer two weeks later received a wonderful letter from the man's wife thanking him for trying to save his life. When Joe did his first year in college, he had been in premed and this unfortunate incident momentarily turned his interest in that direction.

Anyway after that unpleasant intervention and a couple hours, he hitched a ride back to his car and was headed north again. He supposed that the man had either had a heart attack or fallen asleep at the wheel. His next stop going uphill would be Flagstaff, Arizona. Flagstaff was located right on the edge of an old volcanic ash mountain. It was a very small place but it was the home Northern Arizona University. NAU was a small school but Flagstaff, at that time, was a small but thriving community.

Joe decided that he would drive north to Page, Big Water and then Kanab, Utah and north from there. He drove on through most of the night and finally stopped at a small hotel in Kanab. He slept about four hours, got up and headed for Richfield , Provo and into Salt Lake City. He finally stopped at Blackfoot, Idaho for the second night. That accident had thrown him behind schedule. But now Great falls was a chip shot by comparison for the next day. On the 3rd day he drove through Butte, Helena and on into Great Falls. This wasn't as fast as flying, but it was scenic. It was too cool right now to put the top down on his Chevy convertible. He had called Lisa and given her his estimated time of arrival and she was waiting at home when he arrived.

First, he gave her a big kiss and hugged her tightly and said, "I love you." Her first question was, "Are you hungry?" To which he responded, "Yup, think I am." She said, "Do want me to cook or would you rather eat out?" He said, "Its your call, honey. I love your cooking, but I have the money if you want to eat out." She said, "Well, since you have driven all this way, I'll cook and we will talk about tomorrow." While she was starting to cook she said, "Is prime rib okay?" He smiled, laughed and said, "Of course. Anything you cook is good for me." While they were eating he told her about the terrible accident he been a part of. She told him it was magnanimous of him to do all that. Joe said, "It was the least I could do. I didn't know what else I could do."

While they were eating they discussed their plans for recreation, and that they were lucky, as there was an unusual warming trend coming over the next week to ten days which would make it great for outside activities. He asked, "Are you able to take some time off from work?" She laughed and said, "Are you kidding? All I have to do is tell my Dad when I want to be off. Yes, my time is your time." "But you won't get paid right?" Joe asked. "No, I'm the one who tells Dad how much I need." And with that cute smile of hers, she told him that her daughter was with Aunt Lillian.

They talked a long time that first night. Joe had never known a woman who was so easy for him to talk with. Although he was still a bit afraid, at the same time, he was drawn to her like a bee to honey. He was totally baffled by her and unable to escape her grasp.

Finally Lisa said, "I did a little thinking ahead of your visit and I thought you might like to see the mountains and Glaciers in the Northwestern part of the State and if we have time maybe some of Yellowstone and Little Big Horn Park as well. I plan for us to have dinner with my Dad tomorrow evening at his home north of the city. And if you like the general plan we could use tomorrow to pack for the trip." Joe said, "Sounds like a good plan to me." Also Lisa said, "My Dad has a 4wheel drive pickup which has a camper shell on it and a fold out camper that we could pull behind. That way we can stop and camp anywhere we see a picnic table and a fireplace." Joe said, Well, little lady, you think of everything don't you?" She said, "I try. That's why I'm a paralegal by day." At that point Joe made the remark, "You know you leave me defenseless." She smiled and said, "Yes, I know you." And with that they were both tired so they went to bed.

Lisa was out of bed at 6:30 am getting things out to pack. They were fortunate that the weather for the next ten or so days would be unseasonably warm. The temperatures were forecast to be in the 50's and 60's. Lisa fixed their breakfast, and then they decided to go get the truck and camper. They drove Lisa's car to her Dad's home to pick them up. The maid answered the door and Lisa introduced Joe and told her that they had come to get Dad's truck and camper. The maid was a middle aged Hispanic woman, well dressed, about 5 feet tall and didn't weigh even 100 pounds. Lisa and Joe went in and Lisa got the keys from the key rack and they proceeded out back where the truck and camper were parked under the carports. Lisa got, in started the engine, backed out and backed up to the camper. Joe hooked up the hitch to the truck and off they went with Lisa driving.

First they went to the supermarket to load up on groceries for the road. She bought hamburger meat, Ribeye steaks, T-bones, wieners, milk, juice and Cokes, chips and all the condiments, bread, buns and every other conceivable thing that they might need. She also picked up lantern oil, propane; enough stuff to feed and take care of them for a month. By the time they finished all this it was noon. They went back to the house where they packed all her clothes and all of his into the truck so they could make an early morning departure.

By now it was 4:30 pm, so they both took a shower and prepared to go to dinner at her Dad's home. When they were dressed, it was after 5:00 and time to leave. They arrived about 5:45. Her Dad's home was a sprawling one story home, which was about 5,000 sq. ft. with a huge carport for the cars and other vehicles. There was also a tennis court, a guest house and a swimming pool. There was a horse barn out back and the whole estate covered about 200 acres.

The maid answered the door and the chef asked Joe how he liked his meat cooked. Joe said, "Medium, please." Then the maid showed them into the parlor where her Dad was seated, reading the Wall Street Journal. He stood up and introduced himself as Benton Markley. He was about 6 feet tall, fair complected and had brown hair with a reddish tint to it and perfect teeth and nose. Joe decided that Lisa greatly favored him. He weighed about 160 pounds and was still in his work clothes, which was a white shirt, tie and suspenders hooked to his suit trousers. He was class all the way Joe thought. He asked Joe about himself, and Joe gave him the rehearsed version of where he had started and where he thought he was now. Joe told him what a privilege it was to meet him, and that in so many words his intentions were honorable.

Then Joe asked him about his law practice, and Mr. Markley said that there were eight partners in his law firm, and that he was the senior partner of the group. He had been at the same location for thirty years, and that Lisa was his only child, and her mother had died four years ago of breast cancer. He also told him that Lisa did have a paralegal degree and that he hoped she would soon decide to take on law school.

In the meantime, Lisa had been helping in the kitchen and appeared to tell them it was time to eat. They went into the formal dining room and took their places at the table, Lisa's Dad at the head of the table, Lisa on one side of him and Joe on the other. They had Caesar salads and white wine to start the meal and then the main course was filet mignon, scalloped potatoes, carrots, and sauteed stuffed mushrooms, with a very nice red wine to accompany the steaks. The dessert was bread pudding. After they had finished, Joe said, "That was the best meal I have ever tasted!" He then thought to himself, "I'm seeing what living on the high side is like." Joe then thought, "Boy, I've been poor before and I think I'd like being rich better. But, this has nothing to do with my relationship with Lisa. I already make enough money to do anything I want. And when I met her I didn't know if she had enough money to buy her next drink. It's just an added nice thing." And he could not help but notice that neither Lisa nor her Dad were presumptuous or pushy about their wealth.

After dinner they went back into the parlor and visited for a time. Lisa told her Dad they would be leaving early for the mountains and probably would go to the Glacier Park area first and then move further south toward Yellowstone. He agreed that it sounded like a fun trip, and in a few minutes they left and headed back to town and to Lisa's house.

When they got there, neither of them could go to sleep at first. They were both excited about their trip in the morning. They laid there in each other's arms for a long while talking, before they finally dropped off to sleep. While talking, they had gone over their inventory of food and supplies to be sure they had everything they needed because once they got up into the wilderness of north Montana they didn't know when they would be able to resupply again. It was at this time that Lisa mentioned that while in college in Missoula at the University of Montana her minor had been US and Montana history; so she knew already a lot about the country they were about to travel. Joe didn't know it, but he was about to get a lesson in US and Montana history.

They both awakened at 6:30 am and got out of bed, packing the last minute things including toilet articles. They decided to catch breakfast at a local cafe on the way out of town. He stopped at Ed's Breakfast Diner and parked near the road. Joe was driving. Lisa suggested they order what was described on the menu as a "train wreck" breakfast. She had tried it before, and she said they could split one and that should be plenty for both of them. It was comprised of two biscuits, split and covered with ham, sausage, bacon, sauteed onions and peppers, cheese, and loaded with sausage gravy topped with bacon bits and it surely was enough to feed any field hand. Also it came with their drink of choice. They talked during breakfast about the route they would take when they left.

Lisa thought they should drive northwest out of Great Falls towards Flat Head Lake, Montana, and begin their camping there. And from there she would suggest that they explore the areas nearby Columbia Falls, and Kalispell, Montana. This area was in the midst of the Flathead National Forest. And at that point they could decide if they wanted to go into Glacier National park or not. She also mentioned that there were park ranger stations along the way to render maps, pamphlets and any other help they might need. She had seen this area years ago with her father and mother.

By now they finished breakfast and were on their way. It was 190 miles to Flat Head Lake so it would take them about three hours to make the trip. But once they arrived in the area, they would need to drive around and search for a good place to camp. Joe was amazed by the scenery as they went along, noticing that the landscape was gradually changing from high desert to prairie land that appeared to be darker, and also they began to see lakes along the way. It was absolutely breathtaking in its beauty.

According to Lisa, the Glacier National Park area was first discovered as part of the Lewis & Clark expedition in 1806. It consists of more than one million acres of land, much of which is covered by glaciers to the north. This part of the country was inhabited by Native Americans when the first 20,000 or so white settlers came to the region in the early 19th century. As the story goes, and there were others, but the main Native American factions to deal with were the Blackfoot in the east and the Flathead tribes to the west. All factions concerned, it was a steady encroachment of the white man on the Indian from day one. The white man's encroachment on Indian lands was called "progress," at least by the white man. Not to sound anti-white, but the fact is that these Native Americans had walked across the Bering Straight 20-25,000 years ago from Asia before the seas rose high enough to cover that ground and the resulting sea became known as the Bering Straight which was now claimed by Russia.

Joe asked Lisa, "What happened next?" Lisa responded that the US government then labeled it a wilderness, which more or less meant that the US government was putting a claim on the territory. Then they built forts in the area and after the Civil War was over they began to pay closer attention to the area and sent more troops and settlers there. She went on to talk about the Rocky Mountains and the reason why they are called the Rockies. About 200 million years or so ago, people who study these things, archeologists, say the tectonic plate from the west pushed up over the eastern plate and the result was that the rocks from the West pushed up over the top of the eastern plate and that is how the Rocky Mountains evolved or were created if you prefer the term.

And, it so happens that this is the area of the east- west divide or Continental Divide, which runs north and south in a roughly straight line and runs just about right through Helena, Montana. Lisa added, "And in case you don't already know, the word Montana means mountainous." Joe said, "How did you learn all that?" She said, "Remember, I told you that in college I earned a minor in history."

They pulled into Polson about noon and decided to get a bite to eat. It didn't take long since, Polson had only a population of just under 2,000. They stopped in front of the Polson Family Restaurant and went inside. There was a crowd inside, and that meant that many of the locals ate there and that's a good sign. They seated themselves in a booth so that they could sit on the same side of the table like you expect young lovers to do. Since the town is located right on the lake, as you would expect, there was an array of possible fish that one could order. Lisa and Joe decided to try the yellow perch, fried. They also asked the waitress where the camping spots were around the lake. She mentioned several, and one of them was Wild Horse Island about three miles up the west side of the lake. But she said there were other places along the way too. If you see a picnic table and a grill or an open hearth, you can camp there. However, the campsites may be administered by the State, the Feds, or some of them are private. If there is an empty site, you can camp there, but someone will be there shortly to collect two dollars for the night. They will all have some sort of restroom facilities. There are also hiking trails if you like. She was very helpful and Joe thanked her for the advice.

Now their fish was here and to Joe it looked much like a large bluegill bream such as those he used to catch fly fishing back home in the south. They actually served hush puppies and slaw that was delicious too. Joe asked the waitress what she knew about fishing in Flathead Lake. She said there were a number of places to fish; that this time of year the fish would be found at deeper depths, maybe 40 to 60 feet, and that although you could wade, most people used boats to ge out to deeper water where the fishing was better. She said there was a bait and tackle store a short distance up the road and places to rent boats to go to the deeper water where you would probably have better luck.

They thanked the waitress for the fine meal, hospitality, and information, paid the bill and went out onto the street. They walked holding hands for a few minutes and noticed there was a grocery store in case they needed any supplies, but they thought they had what they needed for the moment. Then they got back into the truck, pulled around the corner and back onto the road with Joe still driving. They headed north along the west side of the lake. They talked about it and decided that they would drive up to Wild Horse Island, which was about three miles up the west side of the lake from where they presently were. Along the way up the road they came upon a bait and tackle store on the right side, so Joe pulled over and said, "We need to get our fishing licenses and find out where we can rent a boat tomorrow morning." Lisa agreed. They went into the store and the owner sold them a license, after which Joe mentioned that they wanted to fish the northern part of the lake where the Flathead River and the Swan River empty into the lake. Joe said that way they could start fishing the shallow water and work their way to the deeper water in order to find the depth of the fish. The owner said that there was a boat rental right at the mouth of the two rivers. Joe and Lisa thanked him for the information. They had brought along Lisa's father's fishing gear, so now all they needed was bait, and they queried the store owner as to what kind of bait they might need up there. He told them that live bait in the form of minnows and some artificial bait would do them well. But they might be better off to get the live bait from the boat rental place because some of them might die overnight if they bought them now. Joe and Lisa thanked the man and now that they had their licenses they would go camp and drive north up the lake in the morning.

As they were driving north along the lake, they were looking for a place to camp for the night. Lisa said that Flathead Lake was actually a lake which had been dug out by a huge glacier during the last ice age. Joe was surprised. She said that this was probably about 15-20,000 years ago. The lake is about 30 miles long by 15 miles wide and is 600 ft deep in places. And Wild Horse Island is a narrow sliver of land that the glacier missed pushing out. Joe said, "You really know a lot about this stuff." She only smiled. As they drove along they noticed on the map that there were vineyards and cherry orchards along the west side of the lake. Lisa also said there were apple, pear and plums on the east side. She said she had also learned that they grow vegetables, hay and produce honey and there are some places where they grow wheat and Christmas trees. Joe asked, "Doesn't it take along time to grow a Christmas tree?"

And Lisa said, "Yes, 10 years." This gal was a wealth of information, thought Joe.

Soon they approached their left turn to Flathead State Park. They made the turn and then went to where the camp sites began. Joe drove slowly as they looked at the sites then they drove on to the end of the camp sites and turned around. On the return drive, they went slowly until they saw what they wanted. Lisa said, "How about this one. It has a nice size tree on it and the rest rooms are close and its a bit secluded." Joe pulled in. There was a nice sized picnic table, a grill and a hearth for an open fire. They parked about ten feet away from the picnic table and began to open the foldout camper. Joe said, "I'm sure glad you thought about firewood. I would never have remembered that." Lisa said, "All we need to do is remember to buy some more. I knew firewood would be hard to come by, but we also have charcoal to cook on the grill. All Joe could say at the moment was that back in the South all you'd had to do was pick up some old dead branches off the ground and a few pine needles, and all of a sudden you got yourself a fire. Lisa giggled, "But you are not in the South right now."

By now it was about 4 o'clock in the afternoon, and Joe said, while he was unloading and arranging things and Lisa was making up the bed in the camper, "If we are going for a walk we probably better be doing it. It will be time to build a fire and start cooking soon." They noticed that since they had arrived there were several neighbors who had moved in. Seems that most people want to arrive before dark, as it's easier to set up camp if you do. Also, the Park Ranger arrived about that time. He was very nice and accommodating. He asked how long they would be staying. They said they might be here a couple of nights and he said, "Fine, I'll just come by daily, and you have until noon to be out without being charged for another day. That will be two dollars for today and here is a little book of do's and don'ts." They asked him about boat rentals and fishing and he said there was a boat rental about a mile up the main road that they came in on or they could go to the north end of the lake and there was another. Joe mentioned about the fish being at deeper depths this time of year, and the ranger said yes that was right. And if you go to the north end of the lake you have the advantage of fishing shallow and easing on out to the deeper water to find out at what depth the fish are hanging out. Joe and Lisa said thanks, and they decided they would go north to the end of the lake in the morning and fish the head waters of the Flathead and Swan rivers and then move to deeper water from there.

They went out for a short walk, meeting a few of their neighbors on either side. After they returned, Lisa asked, "What would you like to eat for dinner?" Joe said "How about a good old hamburger." And Lisa said, "Good idea. You're on." Joe had put some briquettes on the grill and started the fire . They got the lawn chares out. It was getting a little cooler, probably in the low 60's by now. Within a few minutes it was light jacket weather. Lisa had potato chips and slaw to eat with the burgers. Joe cooked theirs medium, to suit them, and they sat down at the picnic table and ate. It was not long after dinner 'til the couple in the next camp came over and introduced themselves as Bill and Tammy Richardson from Missoula. After the introductions, Joe explained that he was an Air Force pilot, and that Lisa was a paralegal in Great Falls. As it turned out, both of the Richardson's were products of the University of Montana. Bill was a professor of Economics, and Tammy was a graduate student in French. They had a few days off and wanted to take advantage of the outdoors during this unusually warm April. They chatted for a while and found that Tammy planned to stay on and teach at the university as soon as she finished her MBA if there was a position open. Then the Richardson's said good night and left. By now Joe had built a fire in the hearth, and they sat in their camp chairs and talked. They just talked about small stuff and Lisa said she hoped this vacation would last forever. Joe said, "I wouldn't be here if I did not feel the same way."

Soon the fire they had built was going out, so they retired to the tent camper. They had put all their food in ice boxes inside the camper shell of the pickup. They cuddled in each other's arms for a long time. Lisa asked Joe what his long term plans were. He said, "Well, that depends on you."

In the morning they were awake at the crack of daylight. But they just laid there and talked small talk for a long time. Small talk isn't really small talk because its all about finding how the other person feels about life in general. Joe remarked that Lisa was the only one he had ever talked to that he didn't have to measure every word. "It's the small talk that tells what kind of a person you really are." said Lisa. Joe said, "Yes, and a relationship where you have to measure every word is a relationship where you are afraid to say anything without thinking it through first. And you just can't make it under those terms." Then he smiled and said, "Lisa, you are the only female that I have ever felt the freedom to say what is on my mind without being afraid of what you may do or think." "What it amounts to is fear of rejection," said Lisa, "and I understand exactly where you are coming from. No one can live in constant fear of rejection." Joe said, "I love you." Lisa hugged and kissed him and said, "Joe, rejection of you is not in my playbook. I have known ever since we met that there is a pureness of motive about you , no matter how it comes out. Me, I guess I inherited my Dad's patience and understanding, so I really have no big hang-ups. I look for and see the greatness and potential in you, Joe Ruff." That meant the world to Joe. He hugged and kissed her and they lay for a while longer in each other's arms then drifted off to sleep.

Next thing they knew it was daylight, and Joe said, "Well it's time to get up and catch all those fish." They went to the showers and cleaned up, put on plenty of clothing, unhooked the truck from the camper and off they went to the north end of Flathead Lake and turned on the road toward the boat ramp and rental. It was just a couple of miles 'til they arrived and pulled into the parking lot. They walked in and met the man behind the counter and told him they wanted to rent a boat and buy whatever kind of bait he recommended. It would be a 14 foot boat with an electric motor, which he thought best for fishing, and he sold them some live minnows and a few artificial bait as well, gave them a map and oriented them to the lake and then his last instruction was, "If you have trouble just take the paddle and go toward the nearest shore and put up this red flag."

They went out back, got in the boat, and the store manager wished them well, and they were off. First they went over toward the shallows of where the two rivers dumped into the lake. They were fishing in about 8-10 feet of water here. It was cool, so they left their jackets on for the time being. Joe baited both their lines with live minnows, and they cast them out. They would wait a few seconds then move it toward the boat a little at a time. Then check the bait and replace it if need be, and cast again. They did this for a few minutes and then moved on to a little deeper water.

And then Lisa had a strike on her line, a nice fish because it put considerable pressure on her rod. Joe laughed , "I think you have one, and it is really bending that rod. Just steady pressure, don't jerk it, and every time there is a little slack reel it in." She did as he suggested, and when she had the fish alongside the boat Joe grabbed the line and put the net under the fish and brought it into the boat. "Gee", Joe said, "that fish will weigh about 5 pounds, but unfortunately it looks like one of the endangered trout, and we must throw him back." Lisa agreed, but she was overjoyed with having caught a fish and the first fish at that. So Joe took the hook out of the fish's mouth and released it back into the water.

ACCORDING TO THE DEPTH finder they were in about 40 feet of water. Then a couple of minutes later Joe had a strike, and as he reeled it in, he guessed it would weigh about three pounds and sure enough it was a nice lake trout weighing just about that amount. Joe asked Lisa if she wanted to keep it to eat tonight. She said, "Sure, if you know how to clean it." "Sure do", Joe said. They continued to fish, and they caught several more nice trout that they turned loose. Finally after a couple of hours they had caught and released six more fish and it was turning off a little cool so they decided they had done enough fishing for today. They returned to the boat ramp and returned the boat.

They drove up to Kalispell and found it to be a very nice, new city of about 2,000 people. Then they drove back down the west side of the lake to Polson where the hydroelectric dam was located, a town right on the lake with a population of about 2,200. After that, they drove back up the east side of the lake to the campground.

They drove into the campground and to the campsite and parked next to the picnic table. They got out and Joe started cleaning the lake trout they were having for dinner.

THEN HE BUILT A FIRE and started the briquettes on the grill. By now it was late afternoon and was cooling off a bit. Lisa put the fish on the grill and soon it was done and ready to eat. Joe could not remember eating fresh lake trout like this. But he did know what great fried catfish tasted like 'cause cat-fish is the main meal in the South. After eating they sat around the fire, each quietly thinking about the day.

In the meantime, the ranger came by and collected the two dollars rent for one more night. They talked and decided they would bypass Glacier Park and move on down toward Yellowstone National Park tomorrow morning. After further talk though, they decided on going to Custer's Last Stand at the Little Big Horn first, since Joe was military and this was especially interesting to him. Then they would go to Yellowstone for their last visit before return-ing to Great Falls, since Joe's leave time was limited.

They had been awake since early morning and they knew it was about 450 miles to Custer's Last Stand area, and they knew they had better get a move on if they were to make it there before nightfall. They got all the stuff packed and in its proper places, folded up the tent camper and were on the road by 7:30. They would eat when they were hungry, but right now what they want-ed to do was cover as much highway as they could so as to get there well be-fore dark.

About 10:00 they found Betty's Waffle House, which was open, and they stopped for breakfast. While they were eating Lisa remarked that she had done a dissertation on Custer's Last Stand in College and also one on Yellow-stone, so she be began to fill Joe in on some of the history of Custer's battle in particular because that's where they were going next.

Chapter 31

Custer's Last Stand

THEY FINALLY ARRIVED in the primitive camping area at Little Big Horn in late afternoon. They found a camp site near Custer's Last Stand just on the other side of the river. There were park rangers in attendance and so they were settled into their camp spot well before dark. Lisa asked if Joe was hungry. Joe said, "Yes, I sure am." So she said, "Well, we have ribeyes and potatoes that we can wrap in foil and cook. We also have a can of beans and we can make toast out of buns. How does that sound?" Joe nodded.

Joe started a fire and then put charcoal in the grill and they were all set for the evening. About that time a Park Ranger showed up and collected two dollars and gave them a camper's briefing and a map and asked if he could be of more service and told them where he could be reached if they needed further aid or information. They folded out the camper, made the bed and prepared for the evening to come.

Joe cooked the ribeyes, and Lisa put the table cloth on the table and soon they were finished with dinner. It was now after dark and they noted there were some others camped around them. Joe put a few more sticks of wood on the fire and they went for a walk along the edge of the river. It was April and with the warmer weather, there was the fresh smell of trees budding in the air, along with the sound of water as it rushed down the river bed. What a majestic scene to behold. Soon they were back at the camp and were nestled under blankets in their chares with the fire burning brightly. They were glad they had decided not to go to Glacier National Park because it was a bit cool for that. After the fire burned down, they got between the blankets and went to sleep. It had been a long day.

They were both awakened about 6:00 am by a rain shower which lasted only about ten minutes. Everything outside was wet, but they were dry so no problem. They soon got up and attended the restroom and showers of the facility. They made a fire and had breakfast and were soon ready for the day. Joe, since he was a military guy anyway, wanted to visit the sites and try to make some sense of exactly what happened in this epic battle between the resident Indians and the US Army. They had been given a park guide pamphlet by the Ranger.

Lisa told Joe that the US had acquired Montana as part of the Louisiana Purchase in 1803 and the 1st Americans known to have been in the Montana territory was the Lewis and Clark expedition in 1806. Then Montana became a US territory in 1864. And Montana became a state in 1889 with Helena as its capital. There were also gold mines and copper that became large draws for settlers in Montana.

She said that the battle of Little Big Horn was actually called "The Battle of Greasy Grass" by the Native Americans of the area. The principal tribes involved were Lakota, Northern Cheyenne and Arapaho. The principal battle then was between these tribes and the US 7th Calvary Regiment of the US Army. It took place on the 25th and 26th of June, 1876.

Lt. Col. George A. Custer commanded a regiment of 647 troops. The strength of the Indian faction was thought by Custer to be maybe 600-700 warriors, which was a conception that would prove disastrous for the US Army contingent in the end, to put it mildly. Sitting Bull had done a perfect job of having a strategy and a plan that would make the difference in this rather short conflict.

Before we get too far into the conflict a little history is in order. There was never any significant problem with the Indian population until the Washington government began pushing the migration and settlement of these lands by farmers, hunters and miners in about 1850. The real background of this dispute started in 1868 with what is known as the 2nd Treaty of Ft. Laramie where in the US government guaranteed the Indians EXCLUSIVE rights to the land west of the Missouri River, a treaty upon which the US government would renege. White settlers and miners almost immediately began settling on Indian lands. This made a confrontation between the Indians and the US government inevitable. There was no two ways about it; the US had broken its own treaty with the Indians. It had gone against its own promises. And our government has had a history of this kind of expansionist behavior almost from its beginning.

The US government started a homestead program which, as a matter of fact, encouraged and supported the settlement and takeover of Indian lands, Lisa said. The Indians felt infringed upon since they had owned these land for 10-15,000 years . What the Washington government wanted was for the Indians to agree to be pinned up on a reservation with set perimeters which they were not allowed to breach. Of course, most people who are trying to be objective would realize the motive was to take the best land for the settlers and pin the Indians up on land that was not fit to live on, Lisa explained. There was no way the Indians could make a living off the lands they were left with. Therefore, they chose to resist the white man's advance. And just a small tidbit is that it took only a few years after the white man's arrival for the buffalo population to become almost extinct. The Indians never killed more buffalo than they could eat, so there were huge herds of buffalo when the white man arrived. And all this was done in the name of PROGRESS. So this is what the Little Big Horn fight was really about. And what Custer had arrived for was to drive the Indians back into what was considered their boundaries.

Ft. Raymond had been built about 40 miles north of where the Custer battle took place. It was built in 1807 and there was also Ft. Abraham Lincoln to the South, which was the main supply depot for the US Army. Lisa concluded, "It was not like this battle was a sudden or no notice fight." On June 5, 1876 Sitting Bull had held a Sun Dance Festival which inspired this attack. He felt the Indians had to make a statement.

General George A. Custer

SO LT. COL. GEORGE A. Custer ran right into a carefully laid trap by Sitting Bull and the other Indian leaders. He was apparently an egotistical maniac; otherwise he would not have made the mistakes he did. Having no idea of the strength or numbers of the enemy he was facing, he divided his 645 men into three groups, 1/3rd each under two other officers, Major Reno and Captain Benteen and 1/3rd under his command. The plan was to attack and round up the Indians from the north, from the south and from the east and to herd them thus back onto the reservation.

But little did this man, who was apparently not so bright an intellect, know that the Indians were way ahead of him. In fact, they had been tracking him from behind during his whole march. Instead, they had him surrounded. He finally realized this when he made an excursion from the hill on which he was standing down to the river and saw, to his surprise, among the trees to the north and to his right, a very large number of teepees. And before he could scurry back to the top of the hill, the warriors were upon him and his men. You pick the number, but they were extremely outnumbered. And, the Indians had fire arms as well. Some say the battle lasted less than twenty minutes before all the soldiers were dead.

As for Custer, he had wounds to the chest in the area of his heart, which probably killed him, but also one shot through the left temporal area that was probably just a "for good measure" shot. Also killed were his two brothers, a nephew, and a brother-in-law. As for the fall out, retired General Ulysses S. Grant, who was President at the time, more or less said Custer was an idiot and did everything wrong from a military standpoint starting with dividing his regiment into three factions. You know about the old 'divide and conquer' saying, and he wasn't exactly a brain child at West Point either, graduating last in his class.

Joe and Lisa were camped on the side of the river near the location where the Indian teepees had been. There was a bridge not too far to their left for crossing the river. The weather was chilly so they wore their light weight jackets for the walking tour they were about to take. After they followed the signs to where Custer's Last Stand was; the terrain was slightly uphill to the point where Custer and his men fought it out with the Indians. It was an open space just up from the river, Little Big Horn, which was a reasonable position.

As Joe looked at the surrounding terrain he saw where, under the circumstances and at that point in the plan, Custer did the best he could with what he had. He, according to Lisa, had come in from the north and east to that point on that knoll. "If you're going to have a fight," Joe remarked, "you do want to command the high ground and that part I agree with Custer on. But you know they came in from the north and east and it surprises me that Custer didn't have a rear guard that would have picked up on the fact that they were being followed by a large contingency of warriors. This seems to me to be one of his biggest flaws; that he took the Indians too lightly. And the other thing I can see that seems obvious is that there seemed to be no effort to reconnect with the other 2/3rds of his troops who were only a mile and a half down river. Together they would have been able to stave off the assault of the Indian warriors." In fact, Capt. Benteen and Major Reno had already joined up almost within spitting distance down river.

Lisa said that as it was, after going to the rivers edge, Custer was barely able to make it back to the top of the hill before the warriors were upon them. You might say Custer had the rifles and the Indians didn't. Not so, many of the warriors were equipped with as good or better rifles than the US troops. The simple matter was that of 1,000 warriors, many of whom had semi automatic rifles as good or better than those used by the US military, they were more than a match for Custer and his men who were under attack from all sides and in short order were all slaughtered in a short period of minutes, not hours. No one knows exactly how long, but it wasn't long.

Meanwhile, Capt. Benteen and Major Reno had joined forces just a mile or so downstream and were able to entrench and fight the warriors off for about two days before the warriors decided to call off the attack and disperse. They and the Indian warriors sustained significant losses but that 2/3rds of the Battalion lived to tell about it.

Joe said, "Hindsight is always 100%, but it appears that Lt. Col. Custer greatly under estimated the numbers, strength and resolve of the Indian Nation. Some would say that progress always comes at a price to some. And there is always a perceived winner and loser." "I do think that a better brokered deal for the Indian might have made for better feelings on both sides in the long run, since the life and prosperity of the Indian was so deeply dependent on the quality of the hunting and fishing." said Lisa.

By now they had walked through the Battlegrounds of Capt. Benteen and Major Reno and on the way back to the campsite Joe remarked that if there had been more negotiation of specifics and the Washington government had kept their word in reference to the conditions of the treaty of Ft. Laramie, this unfortunate battle may have been avoided.

By now they had returned to camp and had enjoyed their visit and history lesson. It was late afternoon and Joe made another fire and prepared for a late evening meal. He put the charcoal on and said to Lisa, "What are having for dinner tonight?" She said, "Your choice, hamburgers or chicken breasts and we will heat up some mixed veggies, chips and toasted buns." Well, Joe was forever a burger lover, so hamburgers it was. After dinner they went for a walk around the campgrounds and talked about going on to Yellow Stone the next day.

It was a little chilly that evening as they snuggled by the fire. Lisa said, "I just always have a good time when we are together. I feel so safe when you are around Joe. You just make my life complete. It seems as though each moment with you has a whole beautiful life of its own." Joe said, "I feel the same way with you. I don't feel like I have to be careful about expressing my thoughts. I know you may not agree with everything I think, but I don't feel the least bit threatened by you. You are always on the inside with me." Lisa said, "That is the way I think it should be and that's the way I want it. I've never felt that way with anyone else." Joe said, "Does that mean you accept me 'spots and all'?" She replied, "Yes, it most certainly does." They were already between the sheets, and with that they fell asleep.

They awakened about 6:00 am and were up and stumbled off to the showers and bathrooms. Joe put on the charcoal, and soon Lisa had the eggs, hash browns and rolls toasted, and they had their breakfast. They quickly packed up the lawn chares and the ice chest, lantern and small items and then folded up the tent camper and the were off and running for Yellowstone.

Yellowstone National Park was about 260 miles almost due west from Little Big Horn so it would take them about four and a half hours to make the trip. Oh well, what else did they have to do? They would just have more time to talk. They enjoyed communicating with each other. They talked about anything and everything. They were both deep in thought about what their lives would be like together. The passing countryside was beautiful high desert and high prairie and they passed numerous creeks and rivers.

Chapter 32

Yellowstone National Park

THEY DROVE THROUGH Billings, Montana, on the way west and gradually turned south toward the Gardiner north entrance to Yellowstone National Park, arriving there just after 3:00 pm. They checked in with the park rangers and received a map to the park and went looking for a scenic camp spot.

THEY FOUND A CAMPGROUND in the vicinity of Old Faithful, the most famous of the many geysers in the park. Lisa continued her history lesson by saying that these geysers were caused by underground water that is forced to the surface through cracks in the ground surface by the extreme heat of the huge volcano that under lies the park. They rode through the park until they reached what they thought was a nice spot bordered on one side by a huge boulder and on the other by a large tree, a relatively private spot. Joe backed the camper in about 10 feet away from the picnic table. The were close to the showers and the restrooms. They unloaded their gear, chairs, lantern, firewood, and ice chest and then proceeded to make camp. By now it was about 4:00 pm. After they were all set with the camp, they decided they would take a walk around the camping area. Lisa continued her history lesson.

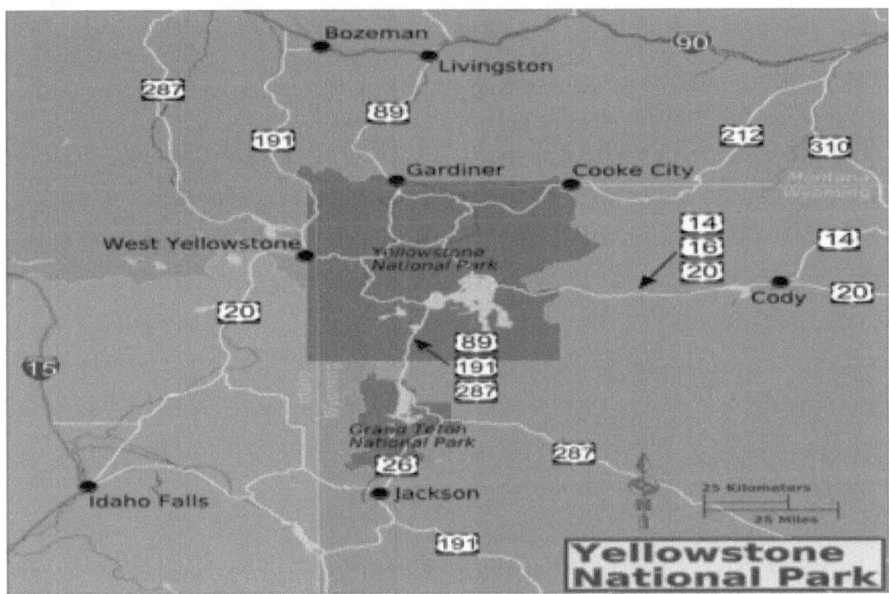

As they walked slowly while holding hands, she started with, "Not everyone knows that Yellowstone is actually in three states." Joe said, "Really? Is that right?" She said, "Yes, it is in Wyoming, Montana, and Idaho, although most of it is in Wyoming.

It was first designated a Park by President Ulysses S. Grant on March 1st, 1872. Old Faithful Geyser has been a main attraction since the early days of the Park, but many other geysers have appeared since then, 350 or so. The trees are considered to be most subalpine and as with most of this country the Native Americans lived here for 15 to 20,000 years before the white man ever showed up. The Lewis and Clark Expedition came here in 1805 . The National Park Service began running the park in 1916. There are 2.2 million acres in all and Yellowstone Lake sits right in the middle of what is known as the Caldera, or Volcano. The park is 96% located in Wyoming, 3% in Montana and 1% in Idaho. It measures 63 miles north to south and 54 miles east and west. It is almost a square in the northwest corner of Wyoming."

Joe and Lisa went for a ride late in the afternoon because they wanted to view Yellowstone Lake and its majestic beauty as described in the literature they had seen. Indeed, as they drove around the lake, it was everything they had been told. The water is a crystal green and as clear as a fine wine. The Lake is 87,000 acres and 400 feet deep at the deepest point. It is a beautiful scene to behold and everyone is advised to not miss this sight as part of their life on this earth.

The Continental Divide actually runs through the west portion of the park and determines whether the drain waters from the area will flow east to the Gulf of Mexico or west to the Pacific Ocean. For example, the Snake River on the west side of the Park flows to the Pacific Ocean while the Yellowstone River on the east side flows to the Gulf of Mexico. Lisa continued with her dissertation saying the average elevation in the Park is 8000 ft while the highest elevation is Eagle Peak at 11,350 feet and the lowest elevation is 5,282 feet. The actual caldera or volcano is 37 miles long and 18 miles wide and the Yellowstone lake sits close to the middle. The last eruption of this volcano is estimated to have been 640,000 years ago.

By now they had circled the lake and were headed back to camp. Lisa continued. There are 1,700 species of plants in the park and 60 species of animals. Yellowstone is home to the cutthroat trout. Unfortunately, the lake trout which have been introduced to the waters eat the small cutthroat trout, which is causing them to be threatened.

Then she began reading from a pamphlet she had saying, "The record low temperature for the park is -66 F and the record high is 99 F. Average temperature for summer is 70-80 F and the average for spring and fall is 30-60 F. The average temperature for January is 1 degree F and the high is about 24 F. The average temperature for July is 71 F high and 41 F lo . And the most scenic highway is the Bear Tooth Highway."

Following the history lesson by Lisa, Joe could see that that she really loved seeing old history as much as he did. Joe said, "You know, history is not just history to be seen and forgotten. History is supposed to be a teaching tool. We should look at history as a lesson of do's and don'ts. We should be able to look at the things people have done in the past and learn not to make those same mistakes in our own lives. Just think how much better off everyone would be if we could learn from the mistakes of others so as not to have to go through the same mistakes and have the same disappointing results and pain that they did. Think how much further ahead in life we would be." Lisa said, "Amen to that." Joe said, "You can go right through the annals of history and find the leaders of each generation making the same mistakes over and over again. Sad, isn't it?"

By now they were back to the camp site and decided to build a fire and start the briquettes for the hamburgers. It was a beautiful evening but a little chilly so they had donned their jackets and busied themselves with getting the evening meal prepared.

ONCE AGAIN, AFTER THE evening meal they went for a walk around Old Faithful. There were quite a few people out walking. Joe had always been a curious science bug, and he said to Lisa, "Isn't it amazing how this puddle of water sitting over this volcano gets hot and breaks through the surface of the ground and spews into the air? It's sort of like heating a kettle of water for hot tea. It heats to a boil and then it blows out the spout of the kettle, same principle. But it is so amazing that that molten ash underneath all this keeps reacting to form more heat; and you know that heat has to rise and when it does, it heats that water which is under the ground. In other words, it forms steam and finds a crack in the earths' surface out of which to spew. And there you have it, Old Faithful and others like it." Lisa said, "I never thought of all that, but it makes sense."

They returned to the campsite, snuggled around the fire for a while and about 9 pm they went to bed. They both slept soundly that night. It had been a long week and even though they had had a wonderful time together they were dog tired. They slept hard, so hard that the first thing they heard at about 5:30 am was someone or something outside the tent near the picnic table. It was just beginning to become daylight. It was still dark but just light enough that they could see a large black object standing by the picnic table pawing at the ice chest, which was still sitting on the table. They raised their heads enough to see that it was a rather large black bear and it was at that moment that Joe suddenly remembered that he had forgotten to take the ice chest and put it inside the camper shell of the truck.

THE BEAR FIRST SMELLED of the ice chest and immediately realized that there was something in there that he wanted. He pawed at the chest until he knocked it onto the ground. In the meantime, Joe and Lisa had sat up in the bed fearful that he might come in the tent camper after them. As they watched the bear, he clawed at the latch of the box but had no luck getting it open. He then picked the box up with his front paws and smashed it on the ground, and it was, at that point, that Joe realized that this bear had done this before. The bear continued to slam the box to the ground until the top finally flew open. Then he sat down on his buttocks and seemed to inventory his prize. He ate the lettuce, tomatoes and lunch meat. Then he ate the cheese and hamburger meat. There were two half gallons of milk. He picked them up one at a time between his front paws, bit a hole in the middle and drank both half gallons of milk.

AT ONE POINT, JOE SHOUTED at the bear and the bear turned his head and looked in their direction as if to say, "You want to stop me? Come on."

JOE DIDN'T SAY ANYMORE. There was a six pack of Coke in there as well. The bear simply popped the caps off with his teeth and drank the whole six pack. As the bear left their campsite, they could hear him knocking the tops off trash cans along the way to be sure he didn't miss any food.

After that incident, it was time for Joe and Lisa to go buy more groceries or go home, so they decided they had had a wonderful trip as it was and headed for home. In another day or two Joe would have to be getting back or he would have to call in for an extension of his leave time. Joe knew one thing for sure by now, at least in his own mind, that he had found the woman he wanted to spend the rest of his life with.

They cleaned up the campground area, packed all the stuff and were on their way home to Great Falls. They arrived there by late afternoon at Lisa's Dad's home. Her Dad was there and after giving him a hug from both of them Joe told him how much he appreciated his loaning them the truck and camper. They stayed and had dinner with her Dad and then drove back to Lisa's home east of Great Falls to spend their last night together. Once they got into bed they stayed awake for a long time talking about what a wonderful time they had on the trip and how wonderful it was to just be with the one someone that makes your life complete.

Lisa was out of bed before Joe was awake in the morning fixing his breakfast and getting all his things together so he didn't leave anything behind that was important to him except her. She made biscuits and gravy along with eggs, hash brows and bacon. He couldn't help but think, "If I was around her all the time I'd get fat. This woman really knows how to take care of her man." After breakfast and loading his things, the last thing he said to her after he kissed her and was getting in the car was, *"I will call you."*

The trip back to old Tucson seemed quicker than the one going. He was back in the old grind and it seemed like going from paradise back into the harsh world of reality where there was an unfriendly challenge at every turn. This was a totally different world.

Chapter 33

Back to Tucson and Racing

WHEN JOE RETURNED FROM Great Falls, he and his friend Rusty were talking, and Joe was telling him about his wonderful trip to Great Falls and the wonderful woman he had met there when Rusty told him that he, Rusty, had decided that he was going to transfer out of the Refueling Squadron to the B47 bomber program. He felt like it would be better for his career in the long run. He would just be moving across the field to one of the bomber squadrons and make a change of missions. "Why don't you move with me." Rusty said. Joe said, "I'll think about it." The B47 had a three man crew, a pilot, copilot and a navigator who was down in the nose of the aircraft. So after thinking about it a few days Joe agreed that it probably would be a good move for the long run. So Joe volunteered for the B47 program about a month after his friend Rusty did. Each would have to attend the B47 school in Wichita, Kansas, which was a two and one-half month school. As it turned out Joe would be in the class about a month behind Rusty.

Joe had bought a motorcycle, but it was a used road bike and that was all he thought he wanted. That lasted only a couple of months until the new 1957 TR6 Triumph came out, one of which Joe bought. It was great fun riding in the desert, but what he really wanted to do was race. This was a fine all round machine. And yes, the group Joe rode with were about half Air Force guys and about half locals. They were a group of about 10 or 12 guys that regularly rode together on the streets and roads surrounding the Old Pueblo, as it was affectionately called. They didn't usually speed, but they did have loud pipes on their bikes and so the police were constantly writing tickets for loud pipes. A lot of these police were just young guys like Joe and his friends and Joe wondered if they didn't purposely harass the bikers.

One thing for sure though, if the bikers were close to the city limits and headed out of town, the cops would lose every time because the bikers would just hop off the pavement and into the desert and disappear.

Remember now, this was before the Federal government decided unilaterally that they, the bureaucrats, and they alone, owned all that land in the west and put up barbed wire fences to keep the bikers and others from using the land that the people really own.

But at this time, there were no fences, unless a rancher had put up his own fence. There were a few situations like that but not many.

JOE WOULD FIND THIS out the hard way one night when he was riding alone. He was on east Speedway headed east and was just at the edge of town when a cop came running up behind him and turned on his light. Joe just dropped off into the desert and continued to move through and around the mesquite bushes. In this particular instance the cop tried to run down a side road to cut Joe off. When Joe saw the cop headed down the side road, he turned off the lights on his bike and continued to ride between the bushes. After a few minutes the cop called off the hunt, but Joe left his lights off just in case. Joe continued to ride for another five minutes or so just to be sure the cop was gone, but suddenly he hit a barbed wire fence. The bottom strand broke, but the upper strand caught Joe and he hung by his arms on the barbs while the bike went on through the fence. Joe had deep lacerations on both arms, he could see that. Otherwise, he was not injured. He picked the bike up. It wasn't hurt. He road home and then drove his car to the base hospital. There was an airman first class covering the hospital outpatient clinic that night and he sutured Joe's wounds for him and Joe then headed back home. Would you believe that all those lacerations became infected? But they healed none the less.

Joe always had been a fierce competitor and before long he was racing in local competitions. By now one bike was not enough. It was too much trouble taking the lights off and putting the number plates on for street riding and then having to reverse the procedure for racing. Joe had a road bike and two for racing, a big bike and a Triumph 200cc Tiger Cub for racing in the 250cc class and under.

Brian Watt, who owned the Triumph dealership, was a short guy about 5 feet 8 inches tall and weighed about 150 pounds. He had short hair, buzzed in sort of a flat top look. His hair was sort of wiry. He was kind of a kid at heart, the kind of guy that liked to watch cartoons with the kids in the morning, but a likable guy none the less. And he was a super salesman.

So, Brian Watt Triumph is where Joe had bought his motorcycles, although it was Rusty Sanders who had also bought his bike there before. There was a lot going on in the motorcycle world around Tucson, and with all that activity it was decided by the guys to organize a club to sanction all the motorcycle activities. So the guys put out the word and called a meeting at Brian Watts' Motorcycle shop after hours one evening. There was a large turnout for the meeting and Joe was nominated and elected as its first president. They named the club appropriately the "Tucson Deserteers." This club would go on for years to come.

Joe was also to meet one of his best friends for life there at the motorcycle shop, Bernie Scales. Bernie was a huge guy that stood about 6 feet 3 inches tall. He had no fat on him and he weighed about 225 pounds. He had sort of bucked teeth. He never finished school past the 6th grade. He and his Dad were commercial house painters who did their own contracting. Bern had been deferred from the military because he had Rheumatic Heart Disease as a child .

He also had a TR6 that he bought from Brian Watt. He was so huge he looked like a gorilla riding a tricycle when he rode that motorcycle. Instead of riding around mesquite bushes, he would just run over them. He was a great desert rider.

Joe and Bernie became really good friends. This was during the time that Joe was doing a lot of dirt track racing and Hound racing and would win the Arizona State Championship 3 years in a row. Bernie sort of acted as Joe's crew chief, checking the bike out and being sure it was ready to go. He was a whiz at mechanics. Some of the time they would pull to out town events with Bernie's car. Little did they know that 25 cent a gallon gasoline would not last forever. In fact, maybe Joe or Bernie hardly ever thought of anything that complicated in those days. Who knows, it might cause a headache if you did any serious thinking.

Now Bern's Car was a sight to see. In those days a lot of guys would lower the front end of the car, making it look like the back end was raised. This was called raking the front. Bern's car was a real street rod. He had taken an old Chevy chassis and put an Oldsmobile engine in it that he had built up and put a LaSalle four speed stick shift in it and that shift lever was about 3 feet long, sticking up above the dash. And that car would literally fly. For its day, it was a real muscle car. Sometimes Bern pulled Joe's bike trailer behind that car and what a sight it was running 100 MPH down the road. That was some car! Of course, that was before the advent of radar.

There was all kinds of racing in those days, both oval track racing, which they called flat track, and what was then called Scrambles racing, which was run on a desert course, probably one mile around with both right and left hand turns and maybe down through a dry river bed and back towards the start/finish line. Then there was what was called TT or tourist trophy racing where the bikes would race on a half mile track. That is, they would race down the front straight away, make a very short turn to the left onto the infield, ride up and over a jump, then make a hard turn back to the right and then a big sweeping left turn back onto the main track and back down the long straight-away. They frequently had TT races at Manzanita park in Phoenix.

Manzanita Park was a beautiful 1/2 mile oval flat track in Phoenix and that is where the TT races were usually held. Joe didn't go there often because it was a fairly long pull for a local Arizona race. One Sunday Joe and Bern did pull to Phoenix where Joe won the Trophy Dash, which was a 3 lap race for the fastest 3 qualifiers. Joe did win the Trophy Dash, but got second in the Main event.

Then there was one other type racing they did and that was called the Hare and Hound. It was run long distances across the desert on a premarked course. A rider would go ahead before the race and mark the course by throwing out lime to mark the course. Finally, all the bikes would start at the same time, and of course the first onto the destination won the race, and these races could be from 50 to 150 miles long. It was really a test of strength and endurance. Joe never won a Hare and Hound. He was always leading, but he always crashed and didn't finish. He just could not keep his cool with this kind racing. But with bike racing, Joe finally found something that was a great challenge and stimulating to do on the weekends and after hours.

One Thursday Bernie mentioned that there was a 1/4 mile flat track race at the Globe-Miami race track. He said it was actually a car track, but the owner had decided he wanted to put on a bike race to see if it could be a success. They decided that the two of them would take Joe's big bike up there and give it a try. So they loaded up the bike, the big BSA twin, and off they went in that Chevy body with raised back end, the big Olds engine with milled heads and a 4 speed LaSalle transmission at 100 MPH most of the way. In those days if an officer saw you speeding, he had to get behind you and actually clock your speed while in chase. The problem for the officer was that when he saw you, you also saw him, and all you had to do was slow down, or you could just out run him, which Bern had been known to do.

The Globe-Miami race track was about 85 miles from Tucson, which was a little under an hour the way Bern drove. Most of the roads were two way roads in those days and this one was no exception, but it was relatively straight and recently paved in asphalt, a nice wide road. As you got into the last 20 miles, there was a bit of a dip and then the elevation settled in at about 3500 feet. It was a little higher than Tucson so they knew they might have to play with the mixture a little. As they arrived at the raceway, Bern and Joe walked the track, and both were taken aback by the steepness of the bank, and they became acutely aware that if you went too high you could easily go off the track and down a very steep drop, not straight down, but enough of an angle to cause you and the bike to part company and possibly injure you and or tear up the bike. So after their walk, Bern and Joe both decided that Joe should stay low to middle of the track lest he be forced over the top. They also noted that the surface was loose clay, and the owner had done a good job of prepping the surface. Joe said to Bern, "Looks like I can keep it in a full lock slide around this track if I want. It's a beautiful track. We will see." By now about 20 bikes had shown up and would you guess that one of the last ones to arrive was Chuck Sherman from Phoenix. He was the guy who had claimed that Joe knocked him off his bike in the creek bed at the Hare Scrambles Race in Tucson. He was not happy to see Joe, and they never made eye contact. Joe thought to himself, "If I have to, we may just lock handle bars again; but I will try to win this race without that. And as long as he doesn't try to block me, I will treat him with all due respect." Chuck was riding a triumph for the dealer in Phoenix by the name of Beetoe. Joe's BSA was running well tonight and he thought he could pull a bike length on him down the straights. But this was a short 1/4 mile track so the straightaways were not quite as long as Tucson, which was really about a 3/8 mile track. Bern and Joe spent a little time fine tuning the mixture for this and thought they had it about right.

Sure enough, in the trophy dash were the three fastest qualifiers, with Joe being 3rd fastest. This was a track he had not run before, so it was a little iffy. And of course, Chuck had the 1st fastest time. They lined up for the 3 lap race, and Joe got a good start and ended up changing leads back and forth with Chuck. This time Chuck was over charging into the turns and pushing Joe wide on the track. He was up to his old tactics again, but Joe's bike was just a bit faster on the short straights. Joe won the Trophy Dash by 1/2 bike length. But there was more to come in the Main Event. After all the heats had been run there was still the feature or Main Event to come. Bern looked the bike over and pulled one or the plugs and looked at it and said, "We're slightly rich. We can get a little more torque if I go slightly smaller on the jet." Joe said, "That's your department, big man, not mine."

THE RIDERS LINED UP for the main event with Joe, Chuck and the other biker, Bryan, on the back row. Off the line they went with Chuck and Joe running right through the slow traffic and into the first turn. This was a 10 lap main event with Chuck and Joe swapping the lead back and forth. If there ever was an evenly matched race, this was it. Joe would pull ahead on the straights and Chuck, with the easier handling Triumph, would push it up in the turns. Both riders and bikes were riding at their peaks. They would trade leads back and forth for 9 laps of the 10 lap race, then the flagman waved the white flag indicating 1 lap to go. At that point, Joe was one bike length ahead so both of them charged hard into the 1st turn of the last lap. Joe had a 1/2 bike lead at this point. All he had to do now was hang on to what he had. They were both in a full lock broad slide and almost 1/2 way through the corner when Chuck added more power throwing his bike out of control, and since they were high on the racetrack, his bike slid further wide and pushed them both over the top and down the embankment on the end of the track, and they both went down. Both riders were separated from their bikes at about 50 miles per hour. The bikes went end over end down the 20 foot long slope and the riders both slid down the slope on their butts, coming to a stop near the bikes. Both stood up, and Chuck looked at Joe, smiled and put his hand out to shake hands and Joe did to same. Chuck said, smiling, "Great race."

Joe said, "Likewise." By then Bern and the other pit guys were there to get the bikes out and return them to the pit area.

On the way home Joe and Bern discussed the possibility of racing the Manzanita 1/2 mile in Phoenix the next weekend. Bern said, "We'll have to look the bike over and see whether there are too many bumps and bruises and whether we can get it ready." Joe quickly agreed.

The following Saturday would find Joe and Bern working feverishly to get the bike ready for the next day's 1/2 mile race at Manzanita park in Phoenix. They had to get the proper gearing for the race as well as the right carburetor mixture with the right sized fuel jet. And, they had to replace the forks because the tumble down the hill at Glob-Miami had bent them so the bike might be unstable at high speeds on the 1/2 mile track. The top speed on the 1/2 mile down the straightaway might reach between 90 and 100 miles per hour depending on the track and racing conditions. By Friday before the race the bike was ready and set to race. Also the bike had sustained some scratches in the accident which required some touch up painting. And there was a dent in the gas tank which required a new fuel tank. But now, after all that repair, all systems were on go.

On Sunday Morning, Bern and Joe departed for Phoenix at 10:00 am for the race, which was billed to be a 1:00 pm start time. The trip there was unremarkable and they took one rest stop at Casa Grande and ate a pack of Nabs with a Coke and were on their way to the race, arriving about 12:30 pm. They unloaded, and as expected Chuck was there since this was home territory for him along with the usual Phoenix bunch. There were about 30 bikes in all. They drove into the pit area and unloaded. The bike looked nice considering what it had been through the week before. Joe put on his racing leathers and his boots in preparation for a few practice laps.

Chuck, who was his main competition came over, shook Joe's hand and said, "Welcome to Phoenix. How are things in Tucson?" Joe said, "We had a few things to fix after the crash last weekend, but otherwise we're okay. And how are you?" Chuck said, "We had some work to do on the bike as well but I wasn't hurt, so we're okay too."

Joe then put on his leather racing jacket, hot shoe and helmet and headed for the track. He entered the slow traffic on the inside of the track and gradually added power until no one was passing him . He then tried it at max performance and speed. By his RPM, he knew he was hitting about 96 down the straight and running about 65 through the turns. By his calculations his practice was just under max performance for the track and the way the bike was geared, but close enough. Again though, he and Chuck would be the main players with maybe one or two more locals. Chuck had come out onto the track, and they were running close to each other in practice so Joe knew that Chuck had the slight edge since this was his home track.

Joe pulled into the pit area and gave Bern the thumbs up. One thing Joe had learned about the Arizona climate was that it was almost always warm with low humidity, at least in Tucson. Sometimes though it could be hotter in Phoenix because of the greater humidity, and it was a little warm today. Joe had run this track a number of times so he was well familiar with it. Today there were a few small holes but nothing to worry about.

As was usually the case, they had the time trials and Joe would have a good time today so it was Chuck, Joe and one other local rider in the trophy dash. The same three would also compete in the main event later which would be the fastest twelve bikes. So Joe reported to the starting line, being in the middle with Chuck on the inside because he had the fastest lap time with Joe having second fastest. The flagman was in front of them with the green flag in hand and ready. He saw Joe creeping forward and stopped and made him pull his bike back about two feet. The idea with being a good flagman is to be sure they all get an equal chance at a good start. The next time the flagman walked away, looking over he saw no one creeping forward and up came the green flag, and they were off and racing. Joe and Chuck took the early lead into the first turn with Chuck on the inside and Chuck almost locking handle bars on the outside. Joe realized he would have to extend to his best performance because this was Chuck's home track, and the crowd was on his side. Out of turn two they came, still side by side, and down the back straight side by side, into turn three where Joe backed off a hare and came to the inside of Chuck. In this kind of racing, if the two riders are evenly matched, he who commands the inside position has the advantage because he theoretically has the shorter distance to go. So now Joe had slipped inside of Chuck to take the pole position from him. When they came through the turn and out of turn four headed for the start/finish line, it was Joe by a wheel length and since this was only a 3 lap race, every single little thing the rider did mattered a lot.

Joe knew it was critical for him to keep the inside position since their bike power was so evenly matched. On the second lap Chuck was able to wrestle the inside position back and maintain it until coming out of turn four on the 3rd lap. Chuck applied full power a little early coming out of turn 4 of the last lap and Joe was able to slip to the inside and win by a wheel length. The crowd applauded the great effort of both racers.

There were 12 bikes for the main event after all the heats had run. The flagman was out front, and there were 3 rows of four. When the flagman determined that everyone was ready, he walked away looking over his shoulder and up came the green flag, and once again they were off and racing. But as Joe was making his way through slower traffic, one of the bikes in front went down and before anyone could react four bikes were down, and Joe was barely able to miss the wrecks by going wide up on the track. As Joe came out the other side of all this carnage, he noted that Chuck had managed to get though as well without getting into the tangle. They both, along with the remaining bikes, raced down the back stretch and into turns 3 and 4. Coming out of turn 4 they saw the black flag which means slow down to a snail's pace but hold your relative position. In other words, if you are in 4th position , you are to stay in 4th position until the flagman gives you the green flag again. This is standard procedure in racing.

Anyway Chuck was in 3rd position, and Joe was in 4th position. It took about 5 minutes to clear the wrecked bikes from the track and there were a couple of injuries, but they were helped off the track. Finally, the green flag was out, and the race was on again. It took a couple of laps for Joe and Chuck to pass the two bikes ahead of them on the restart, and pretty soon they were into lap 6 and now Joe and Chuck began to lap the tail end bikes. This takes some planning and strategy, since you want to make the easiest, cleanest pass possible so you don't cause another wreck or lose any time either. But when your proficiency level gets high enough you work your way through slow traffic without difficulty.

Now Joe and Chuck were both out front with Joe leading by a bike length. These two guys were evenly matched, so bike length lead didn't mean much. It was now the 9th and next to the last lap for Joe and Chuck. At the start of the 9th lap Joe went into turn 1 and was able to keep the inside tight so Chuck could not come inside on him. And Joe led down the back stretch, going into the 3rd turn of lap 9. Coming out of turn 4 of the 9th lap they were side by side with a lap to go, lap10. They went into the final lap side by side through turns 1 and 2. Going into turn 3, they were still side by side. At the beginning of turn 4 of the last lap, Chuck backed off slightly and coming out of the turn was able to get full power and dive toward the inside and win in nearly a photo finish by a 1/2 wheel.

Chapter 34

From the Desert to the Speedway

JOE WOULD ALSO BECOME involved in speedway racing for which he had to travel all the way to L.A., California, on weekends to participate. This race was run on an approximately 1/8th mile track, and he had to build up a special bike just for Speedway Racing. The bikes came off the line together and literally would lock handle bars in the turns. What a thrill.

Meanwhile, back home, Joe continued to race Flat Track, TT and desert scrambles on the weekends. He never cared for Road racing on asphalt. He felt there was too much emphasis on how powerful the engine was, not to mention the exorbitant expense of the bike and travel.

On the way back to Tucson, Joe mentioned to Bern that he was kinda bored with this type racing and had been reading some about Speedway Racing and was fascinated by it. Bern said, "You know the only place you can do that is L.A. It's an indoor arena sport and I'm not saying we couldn't do it, but we would have to build a special bike just for that. They run single cylinder engines, and the whole bike won't weigh over 150 lbs., where here a super light bike weighs 300 lbs. It takes a hard frame, not a swing arm frame like we run. It would be a whole different set up. I'm okay with doing it though. We probably should make a trip to L.A. and take a look before we decide." Joe said, "Okay, let's just do that."

And so, Joe and Bern did pursue that idea. Joe made a few phone calls to L.A. and talked to a guy named Jack Larson, who had a long history of Speedway Racing and was willing to visit with him and Bern if they made the trip to L.A. When they got to Los Angeles the next weekend, they visited Jack at the bike shop where he worked as manager and had lunch with him at a local restaurant. Jack asked Joe what he had in mind. Joe said, "Bern and I are interested in building and racing a speedway bike." Jack said, "What is your experience level and type?" When Joe told him, Jack said, "Yes, I think you can do it alright, but first you have to build or buy a good bike and then you would probably have to work your way from the back to the front. You know how that goes, you'd be the new kid on the block. These other guys are used to running this track, well, most of them anyway. We have some pretty fast bikes and guys around here in the L.A. area." Joe said, "Yes I know. I've heard."

"Then," Jack stated, "there is the bike itself. It's probably different than anything you have ridden. The bikes you are used to are much larger and more all round and less specialized than the Speedway bike. That being said, you can certainly build a Speedway bike, but there are special specifications and limitations as to what the bike must be to be legal under the rules. So, you best know all that up front. First of all, it has a hard frame with no shocks or swinging arm like you are accustomed to. Secondly, and for safety reasons, the total bike must weigh no less than 74 kilograms, which is about approximately 160 lbs., and that is about half the weight, or even less, than the bike you are probably riding now. That said, it must be a single cylinder engine of no more than 500 cc in size. The make of the engine, and brand of thumper or single cylinder engine is your choice as long as it has one carburetor and will burn Methanol fuel. The handle bars are restricted in width to between 650 and 850 mm in length. You also must use only one gear and no brakes. Oh, and it must have an engine kill switch and a chain guard. In addition, you must also have a dirt deflector and a silencer. Now that about covers the bike requirements." Joe said, "I suppose you are able to help us locate all these parts?" Jack said, "Sure. Be happy to."

"Great! Now can you tell us how the competition works?" Joe asked. Jack continued, "We have local competition here and an indoor arena that we call the L.A. Gardens. On a typical Saturday night we will have 20 to 28 bikes here, and they will run in 4 bike heats, and each bike will run 3-4 heats, and we have a 4 point scoring system. The 4 bikes in a heat are awarded 3-2-1-0 points according to their finish in the heat. So obviously the one with the most points wins the event, then it's 2nd, 3rd, 4th. The riders are paid a percentage of the gate receipts. There are out of town events and also team events where we visit other cities, or they visit us." Joe asked Jack if a BSA GoldStar engine would work, and Jack said, "Yes, as long as it could be converted to run methanol."

With that, Joe looked at Bern and said, "Are we in or out?" Bern said, "If you got the money, I got the time!" With that Joe said he knew where he could get an old BSA GoldStar engine, and asked Jack if he had the frame and all the other parts they needed to build the bike. Jack said yes. Joe said, "Maybe we could have it built and tested in about 2 weeks. It would have to be geared for the L.A. track, which was about 285 yards around, but if we raced other places, we would need to change the engine sprocket or the rear sprocket depending on the distance around the track on which we were racing that day." So with that, Joe bought and paid Jack for a frame and all the other parts and he and Bern would soon be headed back to Tucson.

The trip was about 450 miles, but with Bern driving that big Olds engine, it wasn't long before they were pulling into Tucson. They took all the parts to Bern's garage. Then the next day Joe stopped by Ron Swanson's BSA shop and got that old GoldStar engine and delivered it to Bern. By the time Joe got there Bern was ready to set the engine in the frame. They would be ready to test it out in the next few days. The

only immediate problem was where could they find a practice area exactly the size and distance of the L.A. arena? They couldn't think of one, so they finally decided to go out to the old Hare Scrambles area, where they had raced before and mark one out to the exact dimensions of the L.A. arena.

About a week later they were finished building the bike. So Joe and Bern loaded up and headed out west of Tucson to where they had previously held the Hare Scrambles race and unloaded. This was really one weird looking duck compared to the bikes Joe had raced in the past. They marked the track out with stakes. Joe started the engine and made two laps before Bern flagged him down and said, "I think the gearing is about right, but let's look at the plug and see how the mixture looks." Bern said he thought it was a little lean, so he changed the jet, and Joe made two more practice laps. Then Bern checked the plug again. Bern said, "I think that's about right now. It's all set to go. We are ready for the first race!"

It was about two weeks later before Joe had the whole weekend off, and he and Bern headed to L.A. They unloaded at the track and Jack was there and looked at the bike. He remarked that he thought they had done a very good job and wished them luck. Fortunately, they got there in time for a few practice laps and that was good because they did need to change the sprocket and change the fuel jet as well. But after that, they thought they had it as right as it could be prior to Joe's first race.

The starting system was a ribbon stretched across the track which would drop to signal the start. Joe had never seen this before, so the first start caught him a bit by surprise. When the ribbon dropped he was last off the line and trailed going into the 1st turn. All four of the bikes were in a slide, all bunched up close together. He trailed in fourth position throughout the 4 lap race. But at the end he felt like it was a good learning experience.

Joe ran four heats that night and did not qualify for any money, but he did manage a 3rd place finish in the last heat of 4 that he ran. Progress, maybe a little, and most of these other guys were used to this track and style of racing. He would be looking for better times and he didn't mind paying his dues. He thought he could win at this too, though it might take a little time . This type of racing was literally elbow to elbow and it was amazing to him that you could compete that close without more mishaps than he saw that evening. There were only 3 or 4 crashes that evening and he thought that was amazing for the closeness of the riders to each other. These guys know their bikes and they know each other. It looked like poetry in motion to see 4 of these guys riding so close that a bedspread could cover all four.

On the way home Joe and Bern talked constantly about what great racing that had been and that it was an experience that anyone who aspires to racing should see or do. It would be two weeks again before Joe and Bern could put another race into their schedules. Joe really thought that this was the ultimate pentacle of motorcycle racing.

In two weeks, Bern and Joe were back on the road and headed to L.A. to give speedway another shot. Joe was the kind of racer who preferred to gradually cut away at the competition a little at a time until he was up front. He didn't like crashes because the tear up of the bike and can get you hurt too. He and Bern also discussed the fine tuning Bern had done while they were home and both felt these changes in gearing and mixture would make the bike pull even stronger in tonight's races.

They arrived at the arena and pulled into the infield to unload. That night they ran for money and also for trophies. The trophies were always presented by trophy girls in the tightest and shortest of short shorts. After they unloaded, Joe put on his leathers over his t-shirt and shorts while Bern was doing some last second minute things to the bike. It was practice time, and Joe noticed that Tony Mendez, the winner of the last race, was taking the track at the same time. Joe followed Tony for 2 or 3 laps and noticed how smooth he handled his bike. He was in a controlled slide virtually all the way round the track except for about 29 yards of each stretch, where he was straight at the coming turn. Joe shadowed him for the 3 laps and said to himself that the big difference in Tony and some of the other riders was his deliberate smoothness with which he handled his machine. Joe noted that his and Tony's riding styles were very similar in that he didn't fight the bike but rather made small corrections. And doing it that way makes it a fine science.

Joe pulled back into the infield pit area and Bern took the bike. Joe pulled his leather top off and went to the riders' meeting that was taking place now. There was a large blackboard with all the riders and heats listed. They had the riders divided into 7 heats of 4 riders each. The schedule of heats was flexible depending on the total number of bikes present. When the meeting was over, Joe and three other riders lined up behind the tape for the first heat race, and he was on the outside of 4 bikes. This time when the tape dropped, he got a good start and got to the first turn first, but there was no room for mistake. They were tightly bunched. Coming off the 1st turn, he was barely leading by a wheel and no sooner than they straightened up they were already into the 2nd turn and the bike to his left nudged him out on the inside. They traded the lead back and forth for the next three laps with Joe getting to the finish line by 1/2 bike length.

In the 2nd heat, Joe was in 3rd position on the starting line and again got a good start. But going into the 1st turn the bike immediately to his left pushed too deep into the turn and went down in front of Joe, narrowly missing his front wheel. But by now Joe had lost valuable time and would chase the other 2 bikes to a 3rd place finish.

In the 3rd heat race, Joe was into the first turn in front of the others, but he was on the outside and the number 3 bike went to the inside to cut off the leader, which slowed Joe down, causing him to again finish 3rd.

Then it came to his final heat. Tony Mendez took the lead with Joe right on his left 1/2 bike length back. They rode that way for the entire 4 laps and that is what racing is about, polished professionals making few if any and only small mistakes. Mendez beat him by a wheel length on that one. So Joe had 2 third place finishes and 2 second places for the evening. Joe did make expenses and a little money, so life was good.

On the way home, Joe and Bern discussed how when your riding reaches a certain level, the small things begin to matter like just the right air pressure in the tires, and whether the rider puts himself into bad positions on the track while he also has to remember that the shortest way around that track is at the pole position while getting all the speed out of that bike that's possible; and if you are doing all that correctly, is your bike the strongest motor on that track that day? And that applies to any kind of racing, whether its bike or car racing.

Joe felt relaxed now on that track and felt that the next time out could be his to win. He was hitting the groove now. It was just a question of mistakes. Bern said, "It's sort of like Alabama football, they just don't make many mistakes; they capitalize on the other teams' mistake. It's not rocket science. If you can go around that track as fast as the other guy, it ain't the bike or the color of the uniform any more. It's about who makes the fewest mistakes.

Looking from the other side, you can, and you should, capitalize on the other guys mistakes. If you can't you still lose."

It would take several more trips to L.A. for Joe to win 1st place because Tony Mendez and several others would not go down gracefully. It was a hard fought battle for 1st place money every time they went there, but it was, at least to him, consoling that he could run with the best. It took his best effort and all he could give, and that's the way he did everything in his life. He was well known by those who knew him best that he was a "take no prisoners" type competitor. Joe always gave and received the respect of his fiercest competitors.

Chapter 35

B47 School

THE B47 SCHOOL WAS in Wichita, Kansas at McConnell AFB and was two and one-half months long. When Joe went to B47 school, he moved away from The Ranch. He really missed the guys, but while at Wichita he enjoyed the bike riding and the school, though he was just bidding time until he could get back to the desert.

Joe rented a truck to haul his bike and personal articles and uniforms to Wichita. Rusty Sanders and his girlfriend had already arrived a month earlier. They had rented an apartment in town. Joe elected to stay on the base. The first order of business, outside of school, was to build a bike trailer, and this could be done at the base hobby shop. This turned out to be a very challenging task, but the hobby shop had all the equipment, including welding tools to do the job. The head guy, Tom, was most helpful. Joe asked Tom where he could find the materials he needed. Tom said, "Depends on how much weight you want it to haul. 1500 pounds is the legal limit in most states." Joe said, "I would like for it to have 3 rails so I can haul two big bikes and one small one in the middle." Tom said , "Then you should buy 3 four inch rails, an old car axle, and 2 full sized auto wheels and tires and material to build the tongue and hitch." Joe said, "Okay, and we should plan on a 2 inch ball. Two big bikes and a small bike in the middle would weigh about 1100 pounds, so we should be well within the weight limit." Tom agreed.

Joe got all the materials together and laid them in a work space which had been assigned to him by Tom. Then Joe and Tom hashed out the details of how to put all this material together and build a bike trailer. Joe worked very hard on the project when he was not in school. Tom told Joe in no uncertain terms, "Do not attach the tung to the axle without my help. And when you get to that point, I will assist you." Tom had taught Joe how to use the ARC welder. "If you do, you may not get the tung attached exactly square and it must be exactly square or the trailer will not pull in a straight line. It would be a shame for you to waste all your time and mine too." Joe agreed. And, he really appreciated the base for providing the hobby shop.

One afternoon while Joe was working on the trailer, a young lady was watching him as he worked. As she continued to watch, she finally came over and asked Joe if he had a cigarette lighter. Joe was not a smoker, but he did happen to have a cigarette lighter. They struck up a conversation, and he found that she worked on the base and lived in town, which was not too far from the base. Her name was Nancy. One thing led to another and Joe asked if she had any plans for later that evening. She said, "As a matter of fact I don't." So, they met up later and went to a Country Western Nightclub where Joe had been a couple of times.

Funny how certain songs are popular at certain times in our lives and how years later we remember those songs and associate them with particular places and time. The big song that year was "A White Sports Coat and a Pink Carnation" sung by Marty Robbins. He would later die early at about age 65 from a heart attack.

Joe said, "Where is your home?" Nancy replied, "Grand Rapids, Michigan." She said, "My Dad has always been a Barber, and he has his own shop there. Nothing exciting. I came to Wichita because the climate is a little warmer, and I came here with a girlfriend who found a husband here and then moved to California."

Joe and Nancy ended up having a hot love affair. To Joe though, it was just a physical relationship centered around satisfaction of the physical need for sex. He wouldn't tell her that of course, but that was the fact. She had to be the best sex machine he had ever been with. They were together constantly after hours. She liked bike riding as well and they would get together for bike rides with Rusty and his girlfriend. Meanwhile, Joe continued to work on his bike trailer until it was finished. He spray painted it black, and it was not what he thought was beautiful, but it was adequate for the job for which it was intended.

Then there was the flying phase of the training where the copilot got a few landings, but as he expected, the front seater got most of the attention. He was used to that by now, so Joe just continued with the one thing that turned him on.

He did race in several scramble races there in Wichita and he attempted one 1/2 mile dirt track race. This particular dirt track was well known to the locals. It was on an old what appeared to be horse racing track, but there were no banks to the track nor did they bother to put any water on it, and this was an especially dry summer. In one race, Joe was on the second row and got a poor start. Once he was behind, he couldn't see his hand, let alone the other bikes. Several bikes went down in the first turn, and he ran over the front wheel of one of them. By the time he made his way through the wreckage, the lead group of about 6 bikes was halfway down the back straight away. Joe had never been on such a track before. It was a poor track and poorly prepared for a race. Joe saw quickly that to catch them in all that dust was hopeless. So he sat straight up on the bike and drove along behind finishing last. He was just glad to be out of there alive. It was simply a horrible day. The only thing he learned from that experience was that you have to beat them off the line and into the first turn or just don't bother to get out there on a track with conditions like that. Joe would later hope those guys would venture out to Arizona a year or two later. Then they could try Joe's home turf. But, of course, they never did.

Nancy and Joe got along well and had the best sexual relationship he had ever had in a long while. Oh what a great pussy he thought. But Joe knew not to let her get too close; he would surely run if she did. She never did push on him hard during their entire time together so they got along well. When it was time for Joe to return to Tucson, she still was not pushy and this, he thought, was a little strange, since most of his dealings with women in the past had become difficult when the girl began to push for some commitment on his part. She did not push him, but he still could not commit. So, when Joe was ready to depart for Tucson, he kissed her goodbye and promised that he would write her as soon as he got to Tucson. He knew that he was telling a lie when he told her that. He was absolutely horrified of commitment, but he was clueless at the time as to why.

Chapter 36

Back in Old Pueblo

WHEN JOE RETURNED TO Old Pueblo, as Tucson was affectionately called, things were functioning just like they had before he left. The first thing he did was find a super efficiency apartment in the eastern part of town so that he would be close to the base. What he found was a one room apartment wherein the bed folded down out of the wall, a Murphy bed, if you'll remember. It seemed adequate, and it was a new apartment, freshly furnished, and the rent was only 70 dollars a month. There was a shelter for his bike and in those days bike theft was rare, and so was car theft, so the bike was safe being left out under the shelter. He never gave the relationship he left in Wichita a second thought.

Once again, he was back with his old riding buddies. One thing they liked to do at night was to go out about 5 miles east of Tucson and ride Roller Coaster Road, as he and his friends called it. It was a gravel road that went straight north to south, and it had large dips in it so that at 50 miles per hour, your bike would actually become air born after topping each rise. He and his buddies thought that was great fun, especially if you had a girl on the back. It would scare the living daylights out of her if she hadn't done it before. But Joe could not get Lisa off his mind. He had always been able to love' em and leave 'em. They had always been objects for physical pleasure, but it was something different with her.

One of the first things Joe did was check in at Brian Watt's Triumph motorcycle shop. Business was booming and Brian thought that selling Triumph Motorcycles was just taking candy from a baby. He said the camera business was a bore by comparison. By the time Joe had returned, Brian had a 2nd guy working in the shop. It was a busy place. His primary mechanic, Mike, now had a helper and new trainee named Ted . Ted had also bought a new Triumph from Watt.

Also at the new cycle shop was a very short, 33 year old Mexican guy. He was not a brick layer, but rather what is known as a hod carrier. A hod carrier is not the brick layer, but rather the guy that carries the bricks and the mixed mortar to the brick layer. His name was Benny Sallas. He was only 5 ft 6 inches tall and weighed in at about 135 pounds. After some time, Joe was invited to visit his home. He had no wife. He lived alone in a one room shanty on the south side of Tucson. His shanty was neat though, as was everything else he owned. He drove a brand new Chevy El Camino. And his new Triumph was specially painted. He also had a special fuel tank which was smaller than the original factory tank, and it was chrome and blue, Benny's favorite color. Benny also had a lisp, or as people used to say, he was tongue tied. He had trouble with the letters S and Z in particular.

One day, it was about time for the new racing season to begin when Joe arrived back from the school in Wichita. Joe and Benny had, by this time, become great friends. They even made frequent trips to Old Nogales, Mexico across the border. Joe had no trouble with the language there because as you would expect, Benny was fluent in Spanish. Benny always had a cigarette hanging from his mouth, making it even harder to understand him when he was speaking. It took a while for Joe to pick up on his lisp, but eventually he did. They were good friends off the track, but it was all blood sport when they were on the track. For there, Joe and Benny were devout enemies. However, Benny would only race Flat Track (oval track) or TT (Tourist Trophy). No desert racing or Scrambles for Benny. You see, that would get his bike too dirty and scratched up.

Tucson Speedway was located on the road going from Tucson to Phoenix, on the west side of the road about four miles north of Tucson on what would eventually become I-10 Highway. It was a 3/8 mile track and it was a red clay soil with fairly high banked turns. It was primarily a car track, but the bikes used it as well. They would wet the track down really well to keep down the dust, which made it a little slippery for the bikes, but if you have to choose between dust and slippery, you would rather it be a little on the damp side. Typically, they let the bikes run first and then the cars. The races were always on Saturday night.

Joe would never forget the first time he ran the Tucson speedway when Benny Sallas would say to Joe, "You go down infunt me, I wun oh oh Yo azz." Benny always wore a blue scarf around his face with the scarf streaming in the air behind him. He was really a show all in himself, and he was a fierce competitor.

Well, the first Saturday night of the season opener brought out 15 bikes. They had time trials and as expected, Benny and Joe had the fastest times. That meant that Kenny, Joe and Bill Carson, the 3rd fastest time rider, were in the Trophy Dash. The Trophy Dash was a special 3 lap race for the fastest 3 qualifiers. Joe had learned a long time ago that he who makes it to the first turn first has the advantage, and Joe was really good at fudging or cheating just a little at the start. Just like Joe thought, if he pressured Benny early and got to the first turn first, he would have a better than average chance of winning the Trophy Dash. But he knew that first he had to out drag Benny and then simply cut him off in the 1st turn by broadsliding the bike in front of him. Joe came off the line fast and spewed a huge rooster tail of dirt on Benny in the process. It was only a three lap race and there was a no time to lose. Joe hit the back stretch leading by a bike length. But Benny's bike was a little faster, so going into turn three. Benny pulled alongside Joe, and by the middle of the turn and coming out of turn four, Joe was just a wheel ahead of Benny. Joe and Kenny traded leads 4 times on the next 2 laps with Benny winning by a half front wheel. It was almost a photo finish. Joe's good friend and confidant Bern told Joe when he pulled back in the pit area, "Great race, but we have to get a little more power out of the bike."

The Trophy dash was followed by the bike slow heat. Then it was time for the fastest 7 bike heat race. The fastest 5 bikes from each heat would qualify for the Main event. According to the rules set up by the club, the fastest 5 bikes would start on the back row. Joe took his spot next to the Grandstand, and Benny was next to Joe. By the time the flagman had waved his flag, Joe and Benny were already passing the bikes on the front row. Joe went a little high on the track where there was slightly better traction and came out of turn 2 with a bike and a half lead. He knew Benny's bike was slightly faster, so he drove deeper into turn 3 than he did in the trophy dash and continued to get the power on earlier coming out of the turns. By lap 8 of 10 laps, Joe was lapping the slower bikes, and he hoped Benny would get stuck in the slow traffic. But Benny closed it up slightly on the straight away even though Joe continued to ride the turns faster. Then Joe was able to put one more bike between the two of them. Benny got around that last bike, but Joe had opened up a 2 bike lead. At the end of 10 laps the flagman waved the checkered flag and Joe won the main event by a bike length.

This race would be an example of the competition between Benny and Joe throughout this season and the next. The first five places paid points down to 5th place, 10-8-6-4 and 2. Benny would win the season champion ship by 2 points over Joe.

LATER IN THE FALL THE motorcycle club decided to have a State Championship Hare Scrambles event so as to attract the Phoenix bunch down to Tucson. The course of 1 mile was carefully laid out on a spot located about 5 miles west of Tucson. It was laid out so as to have "something for everyone." That is to say it had many turns, then ran across a creek bed and turned onto a long straightaway, then a hard left down into a creek bed portion that was about 30 yards long and then up and out onto a fifth yard straightaway to the finish.

Joe decided to run in the 250 cc class. It would be too much even for Joe to run the big bike class and the small bike class as well. Joe and Bern both knew after walking the course that Joe didn't have the horsepower with his Triumph Tiger Cub and only 200 ccs to stay with Chuck Sherman's new German made 2 cycle Zundapp down the straight on the backside. The Tiger

Cub handled better, but the Zundapp with that new 2 cycle engine that had just come out was too fast on the straightaways and on acceleration. Joe and Bern both agreed that Joe's only chance to win was to be super aggressive in the turns and on the creek bottom. They had heard about this speed merchant but had not yet seen it. But they were about to.

It was a 10 lap race, and there were fourteen bikes on the starting line. Joe and Chuck came off the line leading and Joe took the lead in the first of several turns leading to crossing the creek bed. But when they reached the back stretch, it was a different race. Chuck passed Joe by a little bit going into the creek bed. Joe caught him easily in the creek bed but Chuck was hogging the middle, and Joe didn't have quite enough space to pass because if Joe attempted to pass on either side, Chuck moved over and closed up the space. This went on for 9 laps. Finally, Joe said to himself, "I'm coming by his left side in the creek bed, and if he tries to shut me out, we'll just have to mix handle bars." This was Joe's strategy, and it paid off. They did lock handle bars, and Chuck fell off his bike. Joe crossed the finish line first to the raucous applause of a crowd pulling for the underdog.

It was a great win for Joe but Chuck did protest. He said that Joe had maliciously knocked him off his bike, and Joe insisted that every time he tried to pass him in the creek bed, Johnny moved over to obstruct him. Chuck said he would swear on the Bible that he carried in his back pocket that Joe had purposely knocked him off his bike. The argument was intense, but in the end Joe was awarded the 1st place trophy, and the championship that year.

Meantime, back at the base, Joe had completed his checkout in the back seat of the B47 at Davis-Mothan AFB. The two key flight crew members were the A/C, pilot and the Navigator. They both got "spot promotions" if they did a good job of putting the bomb on the target in those days. However, the copilot got nothing. The highlight of Joe's career was that once in a quarter (3 month period) he got to shoot the tail guns when they were in the designated area, and he had to turn his seat around to do that. They usually flew at night, and there were numerous plots where they made practice bomb runs. The Navigator was scored by the bomb plot on all his runs and if they were good enough, that is close enough to the target and he was consistent, he and the A/C, Aircraft Commander, got the "spot promotions", and what did the copilot get?? He got to keep reading that checklist to them. And what happened when the copilot was due to get a takeoff and landing? The A/C took off and landed the aircraft and logged it for the copilot. That was Lemay's Air Force. Any wonder why Joe learned to hate his Air Force job? Oh, and who had to get the flight lunches for the crew before the flight? Yup, you guessed it, the copilot, that's who. Now is there any wonder why there was always a copilot shortage? Any wonder why Joe led a double life with racing?

There was a hamburger place on east Speedway where all of the group spent a lot of time. They had really great burgers and cold beer, and Joe and his group ate there on a regular basis and were on a first name basis with the guys that owned the place. Joe was looking for a little larger place to live than he presently had and they had two bedrooms and a bath in the back part of the restaurant that they wanted to rent. To Joe it sounded like a good deal, and it was only 75 dollars a month including utilities. There was a cover for his bikes too so that made it even better. And it was very close to Gilbert Road, which took him straight into the base at Davis-Mothan. In those days this was right at the edge of town but a straight shot to the base.

The bike group pretty well headquartered at this little cafe. This was not the whole club, but rather the 8 or 10 guys and gals that Joe hung with, about half of them Air Force. Joe didn't know why, but he seemed to be especially attracted to most of the gals in the group. In fact he had sexual relations with most of them at one time or another.

Chapter 37

Sometimes bad judgement prevails

IN THE MEANTIME, JOE noticed that Ted, that young kid that Brian Watt had hired as a shop flunky, was riding around with this gal from Nogales on the back of his bike. Her name was Amanda Locos. She was, at the moment, living with her grandparents on Grant Road in Tucson. It was said that she was a telephone operator in Nogales. At the moment, Joe had no one on the back of his bike, and one thing led to another. Joe was the quasi sort of leader of the group, and while they were stopped one time, she invited Joe to a campfire cookout near Nogales. Joe accepted the invite and did go to the outing, and they did get hooked up. It was a good time for all as far as Joe knew. Of course Ted knew nothing about this party until she afterwards climbed on the back of Joe's bike instead of his. To say the least, he was furious at Joe for stealing his girl friend.

One of the first things Joe noticed about her though was that she was a chain smoker. Sometimes she would light another when she had just finished one. She drank that way too, but Joe himself was pretty good at packing away the booze. Ted didn't take to this well at all, but more on this later.

Joe allowed Amanda and a girlfriend to take his new Chevrolet Convertible for a ride one day. When she brought the car back, the steering column had long scratch marks all over it where she had struck kitchen matches to light their cigarettes. Joe was absolutely pissed. He couldn't imagine that anyone could be so callously crude as to scratch kitchen matches on the steering column of his new convertible. He cursed her for all he was worth and told her to get lost and never to come back. After 3 or 4 days though, he overcame his anger and told her that what she did was reprehensible, but that he had not meant to talk so harshly. After all, he thought, the sex was just too good to overlook.

Also, in the meantime, Joe had moved into the rental property behind the little hamburger joint that he and the other guys frequented most of the time. Joe had one bedroom that he slept in and another for his junk and a bathroom. It wasn't long before every night was a beer party, and the cops were coming by quite often. The group tried to keep it quiet, but when people kept coming and going on their bikes, it created a noise problem. And of course, the legal drinking age was 21, and not everyone was 21. In later years this would all change, but for now the legal age was 21. Joe lived there for a few months until the hamburger shop had too many complaints, and finally Joe had to move.

He'd find another place to live, but he continued to ride the bikes. Joe now had a big bike for racing and a small bike for racing and a big bike, street legal, for road riding. In addition, Joe had traded for a new Chevy Convertible. He had made 1st Lt., and his take home pay was over $500 a month. He was at the top of his game, or so he thought.

Joe would never forget the Friday night that he had a first date with a good looking dishwater blonde who lived nearby, and they went to the Officers Club for dancing. He had never taken her out before. Lucky for him, she became sloppy drunk and on the way home, Joe just pulled off 22nd street into the desert and opened both car doors of the convertible 'cause it was hot. While they were having sex laid out across the drivers seat, her head on the edge of the passenger side, she suddenly became nauseated and turned her head to the side and began vomiting. That really upset things. It not only interrupted his plans for the night, but he had to sober her up with coffee before taking her home.

Usually when a rider wins most of the time, a dealer will come up with the bright idea to sponsor the rider. Brian Watt Triumph was having the 'Best of the Worlds Race'. Joe was winning most of the races, but Brian Watt didn't want to sponsor him because Watt already had the 'Best of Worlds' rider. Joe, you see, was winning and paying for his own ride. Finally, the BSA dealer from cross town, Ron Swenson, contacted Joe wanting to know if Joe would be interested in riding a sponsored bike. Now you need to understand that BSA had just come out with a big twin cylinder 650 cc bike that was even faster than Triumph's TR6 650 cc twin. It was faster off the line and faster on acceleration than the Triumph. It was called the Spitfire. It had a shorter stoke than the Triumph. Joe and Ron talked a few minutes, and Joe promised he would drop in and see this new bike.

A few days later Joe did drop in to see it for himself. The new BSA was a pretty bike and Joe notice immediately that the front wheel was just a little closer to the frame, meaning that it would be real sensitive or touchy in the corners. It would handle quicker, but be less forgiving than its Triumph competitor. Joe said he wanted to think about it a few days, and then they could talk again.

Joe went back to Brian Watt and told him that he wanted to continue riding Triumphs, but if Brian did not want to sponsor him that the BSA dealer wanted him to ride his bike. The answer was in expletives, "No, Hell No." So Joe went back to the BSA dealer, and they agreed that Joe would be sponsored by BSA. The next season Joe had the edge in speed and power and took full advantage. He and BSA won the overall at Tucson Speedway Championship and also he won his share of the races at Manzanita Park in Phoenix.

ABOUT THIS TIME, AT Brian Watt's Triumph, Joe had met a couple who said they were from Montgomery, Alabama. They were living in an old house in the middle of Tucson that they had rented by the month. They were nice to be around and Joe found from Tony that he had been involved in a motorcycle accident in Birmingham where a manhole had been left uncovered after the city workers had finished working. Unfortunately, the city workers forgot to cover the manhole and when Tony came along shortly afterwards, not seeing the manhole in time to miss it, he and the bike went end over end with the bike landing on top of him. He had a badly mangled right hand which he would never be able to use effectively again at his work. At the time, he was a machine operator in a metal shop and needed both hands to be able to do his job. Even so, he was barely able to turn the throttle on his bike. Joe never liked riding next to Tony because his throttle response time was a little slow. Even so, they were good friends. Joe just took a little extra spacing for the lag time if he was behind Tony.

Tony had gotten a reasonable settlement out of the city of Montgomery for his injuries, and he and Cherry were on a whirlwind trip spending the money. They had already spent a year in California and had decided to stop through old Tucson on the way back to Alabama. They were having such a great time that they decided to stay quite a bit longer than they had intended.

At the same time, Amanda and Joe attended several parties at their house since she was the one riding behind Joe at the moment. To be quit frank, Joe was about ready to make another change though because he had already found that she was completely void of any social graces. Sometimes he wondered if she had been raised in a cave. She did say that although she had eight younger brothers and sisters, she had been an only child until the age of eight, so in her own words, that was the same as being an only child. She did as she pleased, and no one challenged her, including her Dad. Joe knew for sure that he wasn't raised that way but what did he know. All he knew how to do at 23 was fly airplanes and race motorcycles.

Chapter 38

Shotgun Wedding or Not?

JOE HAD A MOVE TO MAKE, and he had decided it would be to south Tucson off Ajo Road and South 6th Avenue. That was a sparsely settled part of town where bike noise was a part of the culture. He was able to find a one room apartment with just a 6 foot partition between the bedroom and the living room . It was just right for him he thought. It was about 400 sq. ft. in all. He had been living there for one month when Amanda decided she wanted to move in with him. Against his better judgement, he said okay. Then Tony and Cherry Crandall moved in two doors down.

Amanda moved in and it was only one week later that there was a knock on the door and guess who it was? Amanda's Dad! Joe should not have allowed him in, but Joe had been taught as a child to respect and defer to older people. What Joe was about to find out was that Amanda's Dad was a fanatical Mormon, and he started out by saying that he just couldn't believe they were living in sin this way. Joe couldn't imagine who put him up to this. The hell he didn't! She hadn't been to church since she was 16, and she was now 19 years old. Her Dad ranted and preached a 30 minute sermon on the sin of living together without being married, and he succeeded in putting Joe on such a guilt trip that Joe promised to make it right by marrying her.

Now in most states you needed a blood test to get a marriage license but not in New Mexico. Joe agreed that they would come by her maternal grandfather's house on Grant Road on the next Saturday, have their picture made by her mother and father and then drive to Deming, New Mexico, and go to the justice of the peace's office and be married that day. And this they did.

Chapter 39

Motorcycle Culture Gossip

FOLLOWING THE ELOPEMENT, the word was all over the bike community. Ted, the mechanic flunky at Brian Watt's Triumph shop, on the back of whose bike she had been riding, told everyone he knew that he had sex with Amanda while she was riding with him. When Joe heard about this, he went down to Watt's shop, walked into the shop and hit Ted with a right hook and knocked him to the floor and said, "Don't spread anymore gossip." Then he went back to the apartment and told Amanda what he had done. She responded with, "But we did have sex. He wanted to wait 'til we were married, but I wanted it right then." Joe's jaw dropped. "Oh well, that's what I get for trying to do the right thing," he thought.

Of course the gossip of the confrontation spread rapidly throughout the bike community and the next thing Joe knew, young Ted was challenging him to a fist fight to settle the matter once and for all. Ted wanted to meet Joe out at the end of north 6th Avenue in a spot of desert close to town on Thursday night at 7:30 for the fisticuffs to put an end to this grudge. Joe said okay, and so the fight was on. Most of the bikers, about 40 of them, showed up for the dual. Joe brought a few of his friends, including big Bern, to be sure the contest was fair. Nothing better than a duel to get to the bottom of a complaint and to get the pecking order straight again. When Joe and his constituency arrived, there were already about 30 of the bunch there to witness history. When they squared off, Joe told Ted that since he was the one with the complaint, he could have the first swing, after which Joe was going to take him down for the count. Then they began to talk through what had happened, and Ted agreed that he had talked out of school and said things about Amanda and Joe that he shouldn't have said. Joe accepted his roundabout apology, and they both agreed to put the matter behind them. So the crowd broke up without seeing the blood bath they had expected.

However, this was not the end to this story. Brian Watt had refused to give Joe a sponsored ride on a Triumph. Why do that, Brian thought, when he could get Joe to spend his own money to win for Triumph. For Watt it didn't make sense. But what Watt didn't know was that Joe had repeatedly been offered that dealer sponsored ride by Ron Swenson, the BSA dealer. So what happened next you only see in movies like " Dual in the Sun."

Brian Watt was so enraged by Joe leaving Triumph that he decided to build up a specially designed Triumph for the express purpose of "taking Joe out." This he did pursue with purpose and reckless abandon. They built this specially designed Triumph engine and painted the bike bright Orange to match the Orange leathers he had bought for Ted to wear.

On race night Watt and his entourage showed up with all the glamour of a show business spectacle with Mike, Watt's primary mechanic, hovering over the new super bike like it was a space ship about to be launched. Meanwhile, Joe and Bern showed up with their BSA sponsored ride, just like they usually did and prepared for the great race to come. It so happened that Joe, Benny and Bill Carson made the 3 lap trophy dash, which Joe won handily because of the extra speed off the line that the BSA provided.

When the Main Event came around, the ten fastest bikes were included. Joe, Benny and Bill drew the back line starting positions because that is the way it was done in those days. Everyone knew that all three of the guys on the back line would come shooting through the holes before the 1st turn anyway. Ted and his big orange triumph was on the next line from the back. There was a false start, and the starter warned the three back row starters not to cheat on the start, as though they paid him any mind at all. Finally on the next start Benny and Joe passed the front row before the first turn like they were standing still. Both of them dove into the 1st turn ahead of the pack with Ted in hot pursuit. The three of them went down the back straightaway, Benny leading by a bike length over Joe and Ted on Watt's new orange Triumph was in 3rd by 2 bike lengths. As they raced into turn 3, a not so funny thing happened. Ted purposely left his power on and went down sliding, and as he went down, he slid into Joe's front wheel causing Joe's bike to do an end over end and land on top of Joe, which knocked the breath out of him. The race was stopped and neither Joe nor his bike were in condition to race again that evening. Benny went on to win the feature event.

This whole fiasco was the work of Brian Watt who was angry at Joe for his accepting a dealer sponsored ride from BSA. This was the childish bastard that loved watching cartoons on Saturday morning with the other little kids. He and Ted almost cost Joe his life. After the bike landing on top of Joe, it was a week before he could ride again, because of Brian Watt and that stupid kid, Ted's total disregard for the safety of the other riders on the racetrack and trying to fulfill a personal vendetta.

Chapter 40

A Rude Awakening

THE FIRST MEAL AMANDA cooked for Joe was barely edible, but the two things that annoyed him most in having dinner with her was that when she took a bite of food she would clamp her teeth firmly on the fork so that when she pulled the fork out of her mouth it would make a loud zinging noise. And the second thing was that she kept a cigarette lit and after each bite she would take a drag off the cigarette.

Also, on the 1st of the month Joe gave her 100 dollars for groceries for the month, which was enough for food with extra money to spend as well, especially considering she was able to shop at the base commissary. Joe almost passed out when he found that she had only 25 dollars left at the end of one week. So, Joe tried giving her household money twice a month, but then she spent all that in one week. So Joe decided that he had to treat her like any other child and give her the household money only once a week. And this would continue for the whole time he was married to her. If a grown person cannot manage money when they are young adult, you can forget trying to teach them. That was when he realized that he had married an uncouth 8 year old by mental age. Now to make things worse, if that were possible, she was pregnant at the end of the first month of marriage.

Joe always was a believer that if you create a mess, you should clean it up or live with it. So he decided that if he was staying, she would also have to do some changing. But there were constant arguments over her childish gestures. She would become angry and proceed out the door as though she was walking home to Nogales, which was 60 miles away. Her parents were delighted to have a full time baby sitter for her.

Joe would never forget the first time he went with Amanda to visit her parents in Nogales right after they were married. He went on the elder Locos' door to door milk route, and one of the comments Locos made was that he was certainly thankful that Joe had come along when he did because "She was headed for big trouble." All Joe could think was, "And now I'm in big trouble because now I have to raise her for you."

The first baby arrived 9 months and two weeks after they were married. And wouldn't you know that three months after the first baby arrived, Amanda was pregnant again. So in 15 months there were two babies to feed and take care of. The first baby had been a girl, and the second was a boy. Amanda did seem to be a little better at taking care of the babies, but she seemed allergic to any kind of cleaning or house work. Joe's philosophy was to try not to make a big mess, and then there wouldn't be so much to clean up. He just couldn't believe the mess that, yes, he had created for himself.

Joe and Amanda moved to a small one bedroom house on Ajo Way after the first baby came. Then 3 months later, after the second baby, Joe tried to get her to take the new birth control pills that had just come on the market. She claimed they caused one side effect or another and so it was that just maybe she, like her mother, in true Morman tradition, was planning to keep having a baby a year until she couldn't have anymore. That sure didn't appeal to Joe in the least.

At this point, Joe thought seriously about leaving her, but what about those little kids? They were half his and what would happen to them? He couldn't desert them. So he decided to try to make the best with the cards that he had more or less dealt himself. He couldn't help but think that he could not have dealt himself a worse hand even if he tried. He now would need to get rid of most of his bikes, since he couldn't afford to keep them anymore. He still had his dealer ride though, so he was able to keep racing.

So now with two babies, they had to move to a little larger house a few blocks away, which happened to be across the street from Bern, Joe's longtime friend. No sooner had they moved in, than Amanda's Dad sicced the Mormon missionaries on Joe. They were at their house constantly trying to cram those gold plates down his throat. Joe would literally try not to be home when they came. If he thought he had been bushwhacked, he knew that for sure now. From now on, as long as he lived with her, it was a constant rub between them. And she hadn't set foot in a Mormon Church for years before she met Joe. But somehow she had miraculously undergone a marvelous transformation and suddenly wanted to be God's child. That is the Mormon God that thinks that all good Mormons will be placed on levels in heaven above everyone else. Somehow Joe could not relate to that line of thinking.

Joe realized now that he had allowed her Dad to bulldoze him into making the biggest mistake he would ever make in his life, all out of trying to pay due respect to the old man's age. Joe was extremely bitter that this older man, a radical Mormon by anyone's standards, would take advantage of him by shaming him into marrying his daughter, whose mental age, as far as Joe could guess, was no more than 8 years. He was angry at the prospect that he would have to, if he stayed married to her, parent her for the rest of his natural life. Somehow it just wasn't fair. But he had made his bed, and he would have to lie in it.

Chapter 41

Big Changes Coming

JOE HAD DONE TWO 90 day tours on Guam by the end of 1959, one in 1958, the other in 1959. Now General 'God' Lemay had decided to disband the 43rd Bomb Wing and send all the aircrews to school to retrain for the new B52 now coming off the assembly line. Joe thought that with the advent of the newer version of the B47, the B47F model, that at least some of the B47s would be kept because it was a tried and proven product. But that was not the case. These decisions are made by high paid politicians and lobbyists whose sole life expectancy was based on selling new stuff to the Government. There was no telling how many aircraft there were in that "boneyard" at Davis-Monthan AFB in Tucson that were perfectly mission capable, even today.

Anyway, Joe was 25 years old now and he was beginning to sober up from the long sleep of the last few years. He was beginning to think in terms of what does the future hold for me, and what do I do about this lifetime babysitting job to which I have sentenced myself. Not only did he not love her, but she made it her job to incite anger in him almost every day of his life. But an event was about to happen in Joe's life that would have a permanent sobering effect on his life. Some say, "Life can work in mysterious ways." Yes, that's what some say.

Joe had also finally had his fill of that man's Air Force and asked to be discharged at the end of 1959. After receiving an honorable discharge, he had applied for and gotten a job at Hughes Aircraft as a test pilot in Tucson. He would also join the Tucson Air Guard in order to keep his flying skills current. Joe had been working at Hughes only a couple of months when he received a phone call from a man named Brock. Brock said he wanted to meet with him in secret and named a particular bar that he knew Joe would know. Though wondering about the mystery of all of this, Joe was there at the appointed time, and the man named Brock came over and introduced himself. He said, "Can we have a seat in the back where its quiet?" Joe said, "Sure, fine with me." After they were alone Brock said, "We have looked at your dossier and we think you just might be the man we need. I see that you have a TOP SECRET clearance and you were recently discharged from the USAF on flight status." Joe said, "Yes, that's correct." Brock said, "Are you interested?" Joe said that if it had to do with flying that Brock could count him in. Brock said, "Okay, well then, there is one more meeting for you to attend." Joe said, "Just tell me when and where." Brock handed him a piece of paper and said, "It's in Phoenix at this address . The one you meet will see you when you walk in. He knows what you look like. Be there tomorrow night at 8pm sharp."

Joe didn't say a word to anyone and arrived as scheduled and opened the barroom door at 8pm . Joe walked in and sat down at the bar. A man about 6 feet tall and weighing about 175 pounds walked over and said, "What is your name?" Joe responded with "Joe Ruff." And the man said, "My name is Adam. Follow me to the rear." When they got to a deserted area they sat down. Adam had dark black hair and dark colored eyes, and Joe could tell this man stayed in shape, not an once of fat on him, and he was all muscle. Adam said, "I have reviewed your dossier. You have spent six years in the USAF, you were a B47 copilot, you raced motorcycles, and there is nothing you hate worse than losing. We also know that you went through B26 school and finished at the top of your class, and that's why you were given your choice of bases when you left Enid AFB and that you picked Davis-Mothan AFB. We have a special assignment, TOP SECRET, and we know you have a TOP SECRET clearance. We also know about you; that you can look death straight in the eye and never blink. It WILL be a flying assignment. Are you on board, yes or no?" Joe said gleefully, "If it's flying, yes, I'm on board." Adam then said, "We will send a special aircraft to pick you up at the Tucson International Airport 1 March 1961. You will be notified of the exact time by Brock. Any Questions?" Joe said, "No sir." In parting Adam said, "Do not bring anything but civilian clothes with you."

Joe went home and told Amanda that he would be out of town on business and would be leaving on 1 March 1961 and she and the children would stay with her parents while he was gone. He said he was not sure how long he would be gone but, he would be in touch as soon as he could. Part of the reason Joe took this assignment was to get away from Amanda, if only for a short while. He had managed to make a total wreck of his whole personal life.

Joe was counting the days, and when the day before he was to be picked up arrived, he packed all his civilian clothes. He met Brock at the Airport and was put on the aircraft. He did note that the aircraft had regular civilian markings. Their flight clearance took them straight across the country landing at Eglin AFB in Florida. On landing he was taken immediately to an unmarked building with no windows. Once Joe was inside he was taken to a briefing room where there were 15 other men sitting there in civilian clothes. They all appeared to be within maybe five years of his age. All of them looked to be healthy specimens, as he was. He was apparently the last of the group to appear.

When Joe arrived, the meeting was called to order by a man appearing to be about 40 years of age. He introduced himself to the group as Gus. Joe and the rest of the group were instructed to use only their first names when talking to each other. The man in charge was about 5 feet 10 inches tall, about 155 pounds with a few streaks of gray on the temples. Also present at the meeting were eight other men who would shortly turn out to be from the enlisted ranks.

Gus started the meeting first by saying, "Gentlemen, we are going on a secret mission which will involve crews of two, a pilot and a bombardier/gunner. The details of the mission will not be shared until three hours before flight time. You will be trained in all the systems of the B26. All of you have flown this aircraft before. This is a TOP SECRET MISSION and no one will discuss anything about the mission outside this building. Each and every one of you have been selected because of your exceptionally high qualifications to perform. The next six weeks will be spent in intensive ground school and special flight training for the pilots. Each crew of two will spend grueling hours working with the bombing systems."

Now just who was this dirty eight who were to, as they later learned, shoot up the Castro forces on that Cuban beach? They were real patriots.

That's who they were. They were known as the "Quiet Generation". They were mostly guys who grew up during the depression era of American history. They were guys to whom their word was their bond. They were guys who never knew the soft life. They were guys who in one way or another put God and Country first. They knew why their ancestors had come to America, and to take it away from them would be over their dead bodies only.

#1 aircraft : Bully Arrington. He was from the great state of Texas, down near the Mexican border. His father was a small rancher. Bully had gone to Texas A&M on a football scholarship, where he met and married his sweetheart. They had two children. He had flown B26s in Korea. As soon as he graduated USAF pilot training, he was sent to Rolling Fork AFB in Washington where he completed B26 transition and gunnery/bombing school. He was then sent to Korea as Squadron Commander of the 34th light bomber squadron. He flew 100 missions and knocked out an enemy train and an enemy convoy and 10 enemy gun positions. He was hit by ground fire on his 56th mission where he, and his weapons systems operator, bailed out and were picked up by a US helicopter and returned to base without injury.

#2 aircraft : John Bledsoe was from Yuma, Arizona. He went to Scottsdale Junior College for two years and then went through the Air Force Aviation Cadet program. He was trained at Rolling Fork AFB, Washington. He was trained in B26s and flew 50 combat missions against enemy trains and truck convoys and gun positions. On his last mission in Korea his aircraft was badly damaged. He had a hit to #1 engine but was able to return to base. After service he returned to Yuma and went into the crop dusting business.

#3 aircraft: Cody Redwine was from Great Falls, Montana. Cody had attended and graduated from the University of Montana. He was a rancher who took up flying as a hobby after college. He then went to USAF pilot training and then received his B26 training at Rolling Fork AFB, Washington. He was then assigned to the 34th light bomber squadron in South Korea. He flew 100 missions destroying five enemy gun positions. His aircraft was hit by ground fire knocking out the hydraulic system. He was not able to fully extend the landing gear. He was forced to make a gear up landing at the home base. He and the weapons systems operator were able to open the canopy and get out just as it stopped. When they were running away fuel fumes ignited, and the aircraft exploded on the edge of the runway.

#4 aircraft : John Shiffe was from Joplin, Missouri. He had attended Southwest Missouri University before entering the USAF as an Aviation Cadet. Graduating pilot training in 1951, he was sent to Rolling Fork AFB, Washington for B26 training. He was then assigned to the 34th Light Bomber Squadron in Korea.

#5 aircraft: Joe Ruff from Meridian, Mississippi had one year of college at LSU before going to Air Force Cadet Pilot Training and flew B47s in the Air Force but was also trained in the B26s. By now you know his history.

#6 aircraft: Larry Smert, Canton, Ohio, finished two years of Jr. College, then went through the Aviation Cadet program in the USAF. He then was assigned and flew B26s in Korea.

#7 aircraft : John Demond, Atlanta, Georgia. Two years at Georgia Tech University. Then USAF Aviation Cadet program. He flew both P51s and B26s in Korea.

#8 aircraft : Randy Cobb, Montgomery, Alabama, Auburn University. Flew F84Es in Korea, then flew B26s.

Chapter 42

A Little History Lesson

YOU KNOW IT'S NO SECRET that the Bay of Pigs Invasion of Cuba was set up and run by the CIA. That is a commonly known fact. What everyone didn't know was that President John F. Kennedy not only knew about it but approved of it and had two carriers with fighter jets parked just two miles off the coast of Cuba at the time of the invasion who were supposed to render air support to those invading ground troops at the time. The CIA went to great lengths to train the Cubans for the invasion in Guatemala, 1500 of them.

But what did President Kennedy do after the invasion, that he had previously endorsed, when it was already under way? He reneged and called the whole thing off. YOU NEVER DO THAT AFTER THE INVASION HAS ALREADY BEGUN. You must honor the commitment that you have made, otherwise what good is your word? Over 400 of the original 1,500 invaders were killed and the rest were captured, over 1,000 fighters. Three years later the US would pay 50 million dollars in food and medicine to the Castro government to get the remaining 1,000 prisoners back to the US.[2]

The Cuban Invasion

THE INVASION OF CUBA had begun in earnest. The B26s, staged out of Eglin, had knocked out all the airfields in Cuba the night before and now the ground invasion had started during darkness of night. There was much gunfire on the beachhead. President Kennedy had promised air support at first crack of daylight. Also, the B26s would arrive back on the scene. The CIA had eight B26s fully equipped with eight machine guns in the nose of the aircraft and two machine guns mounted under each wing, 50 caliber, all of them. Joe was the lead aircraft in the 2nd flight of four. All the pilots were ex Air Force or Navy pilots, recruited by the CIA specially for this mission. As they approached the Island of Cuba across the western tip they were still in route formation, with the number two aircraft on the left side of the lead aircraft and number three aircraft on the right side and the number four aircraft on the right side of number three aircraft. The lead aircraft was slightly in front, and Joe and his flight were about a quarter of a mile behind the lead flight of four aircraft. They were descending through 4,000 feet as they crossed the western tip of the island . Soon the first flight of four would be starting a left turn to the east, followed by the second four. As they turned in toward the beach, they dropped back into trail position, one behind the other, while descending from their perch at 1500 feet to make their runs on the beach. They would spread out in route formation with four aircraft being spaced about 100 feet apart and make the strafing runs against Castro's troops, who were defending the beach from the invading ground groups. Each pilot made the turn in for the hot guns run on the beach. The first flight of four made their run and at the precise moment they pulled off the target, the 2nd flight of four began firing. Joe was the 5th aircraft in line, so he could easily see the four aircraft ahead. He could see there was return fire from the Castro forces on the ground. The second aircraft was hit in the number one engine and burst into flames as he was pulling up off the target. The aircraft then exploded and crashed about a mile inland.

Number three and four pulled up and by then Joe was firing on the Castro forces. Joe got through the run, but when he looked back over his right shoulder he could see that his number four man had also gone down. The remaining six aircraft made hard left turns and lined up for another run. On the 2nd run, the 4th aircraft in the first flight exploded as he pulled off the target.

Joe was firing his guns when he took a hit to the #2 engine. There was a fire behind the engine. He feathered the #2 engine, but the whole engine was on fire. He pulled up from the run and made a hard left turn back towards the ocean. The ground fire, which was intense, had hit his gunner in the chest and neck and he was instantly dead. Joe also was hit in the left arm and leg. He was bleeding profusely from the leg wound. After making a hard left turn to get back over the ocean, he gave it max power on the #1, the left engine, while he slowly climbed south over the ocean. In the meantime, he took a rag and tied it around his left leg to help slow the bleeding. He continued the climb as long as he could. The #1 engine was getting hot and he had the cowl flaps open. Also there was a massive fuel leak from the hit he had taken. He thought he was about 15 miles south of the island when he finally had enough altitude to get out of the aircraft. His other crewman was obviously dead so at an altitude of 2700 feet he opened the Bombay doors and bailed out, letting the aircraft crash into the ocean.

After the bailout, his chute opened and swung back and forth. Once he hit the water, he released his one man dingy and inflated it with the CO_2 cartridge. He climbed into the dingy and the first thing he noted was that he was still bleeding from both his arm and leg, so he used pieces of the parachute to fashion bandages to stop the bleeding. He knew he had lost a lot of blood, but he was finally able to stop the bleeding. He saw flashes of light and dark and things were spinning around.

Joe never knew what happened after that. He lost a lot of blood. He never remembered being picked up by an American fishing boat. When he awakened, he was in the Eglin AFB hospital where he had been delivered by way of the US Navy from Key West. According to the fishing boat operator, he had been found floating in the ocean, appearing to them to be dead. Only after getting to the dingy did the fishing boat captain realize that Joe was still alive. They rushed him to the Navy facility in Key West and after transfusing four units of blood, they transferred him to Eglin AFB. Joe had no recollection from the time he hit the water until after the blood transfusion.

Chapter 43

Meanwhile, Back in Tucson

WHEN JOE GOT OUT OF the hospital, he returned to Tucson and went back to work at his job with Hughes Aircraft even though he had not yet completely recovered from the injuries he had sustained in the Cuba invasion. It would take a little longer in rehab for him to get back on flying status with the Arizona Air Guard. He was depressed and saddened by the fact that he had almost lost his life while his friends did lose theirs, and at the same time he was angry that President Kennedy had pulled the rug out from under all of them after the invasion had already begun, showing his reckless disregard for Joe's life, as well as the others who had perished in the failed attempt to liberate Cuba from Castro.

During his recovery, Joe had had a lot of time for reflection and felt intense contempt for a father-in-law who had used trickery and deception to more or less shotgun wed Joe to his daughter. So on his return to Tucson, he was in no frame of mind to be pushed or abused in any way. As far as he was concerned, he had systematically made the wrong decisions regarding all the major things that a responsible adult person is supposed to make. He realized that his parents had so many problems of their own, and they were two very immature people, that they failed to teach him or give him the tools to make major decisions in life, like who should he marry and why he should marry that person. All of the relationships he had before were superficial and based on the physical need for sexual gratification, with one notable exception, Lisa. But she was two and a half years in the rear view mirror now, so probably too late for that. And he had heard his Dad say before that "A hard Dick hath no conscience", which is not meant to offend anyone, its just a matter of fact with most young guys. It's just a fact that most young men are out for sexual or physical gratification the same as a Buck deer. In most cases there is no other intent on the man's part, that is most of the time. But now and then there appears a special woman like Lisa, who is totally different, and that's where the buck stops.

Joe thought long and hard about what his next move in this life saga was to be. Not having the experience or advice from others that would be credible, he just didn't know which way to turn. He still had a limp and was still recovering from his injuries to his left arm and leg. His arm seemed to be doing better, but then he didn't have to walk on it. He was still not quite ready to return to flight status.

He knew that his relationship with Amanda continued to be on an adult to child basis. Her own mother had made the comment to her friends at Amanda's baby shower that her husband was good for her because he wouldn't let her get away with things that she and her father did. In other words, her husband was a strong disciplinarian where her parents were not. Now isn't that a hell of a way to live? How long could he put up with the tantrums that she threw? He was torn. Do I just accept that we will have an adult to child relationship for the next fifty or sixty years or do I take the bull by the horns and make the permanent change that seems obvious? Do I make a change for the survival of my own sanity or do I toe the line, surrender myself to a lifetime of unhappiness that I can see awaits me, including having the Mormon church crammed down my throat, a slave to a marriage of insanity? Joe and Amanda never talked about anything. He was stuck with the job of dictating to an 8 year old and taking responsibility of two babies as well . It was a living hell.

Finally, after a few more months, he decided the only way to keep his sanity was to get out of the marriage. He hated this because he now had two babies who were 15 months apart. But he knew he could not continue with Amanda and her Dad and keep his sanity. He was always preoccupied with his contempt for her and her Dad, so he decided that he had to make a move. He called her Dad on the telephone and requested that he come to their home for a meeting. When he arrived, Joe thought he seemed defensive. Joe started by saying that her Dad had more or less made this a shotgun wedding and that even though Joe was not a proponent of divorce, he would be separating from Amanda and suing for divorce. Joe went on to say that he himself deserved a large part of the blame because he should have picked up on the signs earlier and should never have become involved with her. However, he would never have become deeply involved if Martin, her father, had not caught Joe off guard by showing up at Joe's house uninvited. Joe went on to say, "Then you sicced the Mormon missionaries on me to make a bad situation worse. I can't help it that your daughter's mental age is 8 years old. You and her mother are to blame for that in not teaching her to accept her younger siblings in an unchallenged but loving way. Be that as it may, she has a mental age of 8. I cannot and will not spend the rest of my life raising your daughter. You are getting her back. I am not leaving her or you without recourse though. I will render child support to my children through age 18, and I will send both of them to the college of their choice should they choose to attend. I am taking my personal effects to another location today, and Amanda will hear from my lawyer. I wish neither you nor Amanda any ill will, but you all will have to work out your problems without my presence. I will have nothing to do with you after today. I would like to visit my children from time to time if the details can be worked out, and I will still carry the children on my medical insurance for as long as I can." Martin started to make a rebuttal, but Joe held up his hand and said, "Save it for the court, if you choose to do so. I'm out of here!" And at that point, Joe stood up, ending the meeting, and began to gather up his belongings.

As soon as Joe was settled in his small but adequate apartment, the first thing he thought about was Lisa. It had now been two and a half years since he left her in Great Falls, Montana telling her he would call her. Joe figured she had long since moved on. But since she was the only woman he had ever loved, he picked up the phone and called her number. She answered and he said, *"Hi Lisa, this is Joe."* And Lisa said, *"Hi there. I've been waiting for your call."*

---

[1]Just a little history here is in order. The Aleutian Islands are an archipelago or

archipelago or semi-circle of islands protruding off the southwest coast of Alaska curving towards Russia. Ownership of the islands is claimed in part by the US and Russia. There are about 150 of these islands, most of which are volcanic. They separate the North Pacific Ocean from the Bering Sea. This, if one is a history buff, is where first life in the US crossed from Siberia to the North American Continent some 10,000 plus years ago. At that time the sea level was low enough that the first people to come to North America were able to simply walk across.

[2] How about another little history lesson? Let us fast forward from 17 April 1961 to 22 November 1963. Let us just assume that Lee Harvey Oswalt was the lone assassin of President John F. Kennedy. Are you aware that Lee Harvey Oswalt's two best friends at the time of Kennedy's assassination were both undercover CIA operatives? They were. Do you remember Oswalt telling the Dallas Police that he was "just a patsy." Do you also remember that Jack Ruby, who shot and killed Oswalt, had a long occult relationship with the CIA, and the man who owned the Texas book depository was a Kennedy hater and that the parade route was changed just two hours before parade time so that it would come by the Book depository? Well, it was. And wasn't it strange that Vice President Lyndon Johnson just happened to be in Dallas that day, but was not part of the parade? But, he was close enough to run and jump onto Air Force One and have himself sworn in as President immediately after Kennedy was pronounced dead at Parkland hospital.

And the investigation panel that he handpicked himself found Lee Harvey Oswalt to be a lone wolf killer of the President of the United States. Do you really think that Lee Harvey Oswalt was intelligent enough to plan and pull off this whole event alone? Would it be presumptuous to think that someone else might have helped him plan and execute this event? And don't you think this panel, appointed by the newly sworn-in President, Lyndon Baines Johnson, knew more than they told the American people? A whole lot of Deep State Operation was going on.

Now you don't have to be Sherlock Holmes to think, "Here is a boy, an ex marine private, who figured out all these details of how to be at the right place at exactly the right time to do his dirty work and slip out of the building unnoticed. And he also knew the parade route in time to get in precisely the correct position. And he was a Marine sharp shooter. And that Jack Ruby just happened to kill Oswalt before he had time to talk." If you believe this, then you are a bigger "patsy" than Oswalt.

The CIA has always said, give me a mission and a "plausible" denial and I can do it. Most of the American public apparently bought the whole thing hook, line and sinker. When double crossed, the CIA will get even, and they did. Where was Lynden Baines Johnson that day? Right there in Dallas. Where was Poppy Bush, head of the FBI? 100 miles away in Tyler, Texas, with Barbara getting her hare done. Everyone who could potentially be affected was close by.

Don't miss out!

Click the button below and you can sign up to receive emails whenever P.T. "Doc" Carney publishes a new book. There's no charge and no obligation.

https://books2read.com/r/B-A-LHVF-CSCS

BOOKS 2 READ

Connecting independent readers to independent writers.

About the Author

P.T. "Doc" Carney has entered the Golden Age of Retirement and is finally able to realize his dream of writing and publishing novels that he has envisioned for many years.

He is a retired USAF pilot, who entered cadet training at the end of the Korean War and then flew with the Mississippi Air Guard for many years as a pilot and then as flight surgeon after receiving his medical license.

He grew up in Rural Mississippi and as a child with ADHD was misunderstood for most of his childhood, as there was no diagnosis for ADHD at that time. He later specialized in child psychiatry to address some of these issues.

But he writes about the 1930s through the 1960s as the Golden Era in America and is very proud of his experiences throughout that time.

He offers here an overall view of those early days through the eyes of one Joe Ruff.

Photo courtesy of MidAmerica Auctions